Good News?

After working for Pepsi, *Hindustan Times* and ACNielsen for ten years, Zarreen Khan decided to take a break and raise two children, who are sometimes kind enough to let her role-play as a marketing consultant. She lives in Delhi with her husband, dealing with the craziness of being half-Muslim and half-Punjabi, which is detrimental to her weight, sanity and sense of humour. Zarreen's first book, *I Quit, Now What?*, was published in 2017. This is her second book.

Koi Good News?

ZARREEN KHAN

HarperCollins *Publishers* India

First published in India by
HarperCollins *Publishers* in 2018
A-75, Sector 57, Noida, Uttar Pradesh 201301, India
www.harpercollins.co.in

2 4 6 8 10 9 7 5 3 1

Copyright © Zarreen Khan 2018

P-ISBN: 978-93-5277-905-5
E-ISBN: 978-93-5277-906-2

Typeset in 11/14.1 Minion Pro
Manipal Digital Systems, Manipal

Printed and bound at
Thomson Press (India) Ltd

For Kyrah, Zayn and Iram

Week LMP (Last Menstrual Period before pregnancy) minus 4

A woman's fertility begins to decline after the age of thirty

Mona

The most chaotic afternoon ever in the Amritsar household.

Had to spend three and a half hours with Daisy chachi, trying to convince her that Nishi bua had not stolen her outfit design on purpose. Daisy chachi is distraught. Apparently she had the *chungi ka* tailor spend weeks copying the design she saw her daughter-in-law's sister's mother-in-law wear at a wedding in Delhi. And now the so-called evil Nishi bua has got herself the exact same outfit made and is planning to wear it tonight.

We had to drag Daisy chachi out of the room before her verbal assault turned physical, while Nishi bua sat unperturbed, tying up the little bags of besan ke laddoos, which are to be sent to the boy's side tomorrow as shagan.

I'm not sure why Mummy left me in charge of pacifying the volcanic Daisy chachi (perhaps because I'm the only sensible woman in this family), but there I was, locked up in my room, making sympathetic tutting noise to calm down a furious Daisy chachi. She's been watching a soap too many on Star Plus, if you ask me. She believes it's some grand Deol family saazish against her, because at cousin

3

Mohini's engagement, she wore the same polki set (which we know was fake) that Nishi bua wanted to wear (which we also know was fake). So this, she believed, was Nishi bua's way of taking revenge.

They both hate each other. Have for years. It started out during their schooldays, when both Nishi bua and Daisy chachi harboured 'feelings' for the same rich halwai ka beta, who kept them both hanging, only to marry that Jams and Cakes wale ki daughter, leaving them both heartbroken, and locked in some everlasting competition. Mummy's told me all about it. Mummy claims she's not one for gossip, but one week of being married into this family and I knew my mother-in-law was bursting at the seams with 'information'.

So un-school-principal-like. That's what she was till last year, my husband Ramit's mother. Principal of an all-girls convent school in Amritsar. I've never met someone who looks the part more than her. She's always in these starched cotton saris, with perfectly pleated pallas, big bindi on her large forehead, glasses atop her head, hair in an oh-so-school-teacher-type 'blunt cut'. Very unlike my own mother, who's petite and disorganized, her frizzy hair pulled back in a messy ponytail, paddling around in her unmatched salwar-kameez suits. She looks quite 'bechari'. Highly deceptive, of course. Because she's really just as much a tigress as my mother-in-law.

For two whole hours, Daisy chachi bored me with her theories and even hinted at Mummy being a part of the conspiracy, till Mummy walked in and scorched her with one solid principal-like stare. No one messes with Mummy.

Anyway, after a while, they settled for a truce, since it is, after all, apni Chiku's wedding. A somewhat friendly compromise to wear matching outfits tonight has been reached. It will now be a battle of who's pairing it with better jewellery – and who's looking slimmer. Daisy chachi has scurried off with her daughter-in-law to the locker. And for liposuction, maybe.

I should've expected it, though. It's a Deol wedding. Deol weddings are loud, boisterous, often violent and always a circus.

Four years ago, at my own wedding, I was nothing less than horrified to discover that my lovely, docile, serious Ramit belonged to *this* Sooraj Barjatya consortium. Sixteen first cousins. Twenty-two second cousins. God knows how many thirds. And that's only on the paternal side. Everyone we meet on the Amritsar streets is somehow related to us. Bua's husband's cousin's son. Maasi's daughter's husband's brother. Cousin's mother-in-law's sister's husband. They don't have a family tree. They have a family forest.

Ramit calls the cousins 'bheed'. I thought it was pretty rude initially, but there's no other way to describe it. The rhyming names, the cacophony of guttural laughter, the free-flow of alcohol, the non-stop cricket in the driveway, the daily fashion show. They're all just loud, happy Punjabis. *We* are, I mean. I am one of them now.

Anyway, back to the point … after the truce, we returned to meet the inflow of relatives arriving for Chiku's wedding, and I was subjected to a fresh bout of the same conversation: *arrey! Looking nice and healthy! Looking fully Punjabi like us now! Where is Ramit? What are you doing nowadays? When are you 'planning'?*

Planning. How I've come to hate that word.

After all, four years of marriage and no baby. No 'good news'.

And Ramit has sent me here to face this ALONE!

Ramit

Eight texts. In one hour. While I'm in a meeting with a client.

I'd told Mona to message me only if things were urgent. And there are eight messages. In one hour.

Finally, had to put my phone on silent after Surjit shot me a 'pay attention' look.

I have to stop feeling guilty about sending her to Amritsar alone.

Mona

Chill? Chill??? That's all he had to say???

Sent him another one:

Eight people have asked me the question. Eight! Koi good news? Somesh tayi even ran her hand around my paunch saying bata bhi de. I know I've put on a little bit of weight but to mistake it for a baby? Then Nishi bua asked whether we are planning. Then Suttu asked. Suttu, aged eighteen, who should be concentrating on her exams rather than our 'good news'! Then some neighbour I've never seen before asked me if I was Kavita's bahu, the Delhi one, who doesn't have any children yet. That's how they describe me! How could you send me here alone? How could you? And don't you ever say chill to me again!

His response after five whole minutes: *k*

And then nothing.

I stuffed my phone into my pocket after that. There is no point in fuming over it. Because it's Ramit.

For four years I have had the sole responsibility of keeping conversations alive in our household. When he gets back from office, I tell him everything that has happened in my life. Everything. The maid came. The maid said. The maid cooked. The maid complained. The maid quit. Mom called. Mom said. Mom complained. Mom slammed the phone down. Mummy called. Mummy said. Mummy complained. Mummy advised.

Ramit's response: *K*

He doesn't even bother with prefixing an O any more!

Now that's us: I talk. He says K.

Was it like this when we weren't married? I can no longer remember. He was never much of a talker, but to be reduced to a single alphabet? Most days, he stays buried in his phone or his laptop, his mind on his newly set-up business and his conversations as crisp as his business emails. It's like he has no emotions.

I told him exactly that, though in slightly more detail, through yet another SMS, and hit SEND right before Dadi called me for a status update on the Daisy chachi–Nishi bua brawl.

Ramit

Yet another message from Mona. She was conned into a meeting with Dadi, supposedly for a conversation on some sort of fight chachi and bua were engaged in, but it turned out to be a conversation on our family planning.

Advanced my tickets to tomorrow lest my family becomes the reason for my divorce.

Mona

I wish I could be more like Ramit at times like these. Ramit would've just said 'no plan' and walked off. I just sat there, red-faced. But then to be fair, these conversations embarrass Ramit more than they embarrass me. It also shows a whole lot more on his Punjabi complexion.

Oh these conversations!

When we married at the ripe old-age of twenty-seven, we thought we had finally escaped the 'when are you getting married' phase. But waiting for me – for us – on the other side, was the dark demon of 'good news'.

Ramit would snap, saying, 'We just got married, isn't that enough good news?' But apparently wedding *toh honi hi thhi*. Now give us the 'real' good news – that your reproductive organs are working.

We skirted the issue pretty successfully initially ... or so feels the innocent-to-the-extent-of-being-dumb Ramit. I, of course, disagree.

We used a gamut of excuses.

Abhi hum ek doosre ko jaan le: Which was, okay, a slightly lame excuse. We had a love marriage. But trust the Deols to come back with the clichéd 'you have the rest of your life to get to know each other.'

Abhi humari umar hi kya hai: A fairly valid excuse at twenty-seven. Apparently not at twenty-eight. Not only is my biological clock ticking, it is also a point of prolonged discussion.

Abhi humein duniya dekhni hai: Okay, fine, that does sound like Kajol from *DDLJ*. We heard a lot of gasps at that one. How dare we put ourselves before their to-be grandchild/ niece/nephew! I think Ramit's Dadi fainted.

Abhi hum financially stable nahin hain: We seriously couldn't afford a kid. We always got a: 'So what? We couldn't afford kids either. In fact, we didn't even get as much salary as you guys do nowadays.' Which is seriously rubbish! Delivery at their times would cost them 200 bucks and it now costs you 2,00,000.

The truth is, we really didn't want kids till last year. Ramit was setting up his business, we were staying in a rented house, and we had very little saved up. The idea of the expenses that come with a baby scared us. Not to mention the responsibility.

There were some people who were kind enough to say: 'It's only your first year of marriage – enjoy yourself.' I actually fell for this sugar-coated talk. They were the first ones to call us on our first anniversary and say, '*Ab toh khoob enjoy kar liya. Ab toh good news suna do.*' Clearly our 'enjoyment' needed to *end* by giving them 'good news' quickly!

And in our second year of marriage, every Tom, Dick and Harry believed it was their right to discuss our sex life. And of course, it's only out of kindness and concern regarding our conception issues. Because we guys *do* have conception issues, right? No other reason we're not reproducing?

So be it the aunts and uncles or the bhabis and chachis, or the maids who stopped whispering the minute I entered the kitchen, or even the colony aunties whose main occupation otherwise is to stand in their balconies displaying their non-dupatted cleavage and whose claim to fame had been Bittu-ke-papa getting them pregnant within two months of their marriage – my baby-producing skills were being questioned at large. And still are.

And there was the biggest issue of it all – being a Deol. The Deol family of Punjab is as fertile as the soil they sing songs about. We seem to have broken some generation-old tradition by not reproducing almost immediately after marriage. Since Ramit is a Deol, obviously the fertility problem can't lie with him. So it's me who everyone reserves those looks for.

Ramit

We couldn't afford to have kids. Period. Don't know why Mona can't tell them exactly that.

Sometimes I wish I had warned her about the bheed before we got married. To think of it, it was slightly evil to get Mummy-Papa to meet Mona and her family in her house in Dehradun rather than let them come and see the wildlife resort we live in. Mona had innocently thought that since I was the only child, it was just Mummy-Papa and me.

But then again, Mona should have understood when I told her the baraat would be 500 people, and that it was best we had the ceremonies in Amritsar. What did she expect? 500 friends?

Mona

So finally I'm meandering my way through the bheed, carrying in my arms the mewa ki dibbis that Chiku wants us to distribute during the pheras like she saw on some Pakistani show, when Mohini arrives with her post-honeymoon glow, her sindoor running down her forehead, her chura clanging as she hugs the junta and then, red-faced, announces she's pregnant.

My brain goes into overdrive. How! She has only been married one and a half months! I'm sure they'd been up to something before the wedding, otherwise there is no way this could have happened. I steal a glance at Mummy, who's clearly frozen in shock. She's probably mulling over the same conspiracy theory. Then I realize that a lot of people are stealing glances at me in return. I suddenly felt very hot.

Toshi, the only one in the same boat as me, since she hasn't given 'good news' in the one year she's been married, (though she's twenty-five, and six years younger than me) tells me in hushed tones, *'Arrey! Kya jaldi thhi?* Can't they keep their hands off each other?'

But I think Mummy's had enough now. She takes me up to my room, shuts the door discreetly, sits me down, wears her best school-principal expression and asks me seriously what the 'progress' is. I am mortified by these conversations. I keep thinking she is picturing me having sex. She's even told me a couple of times how I need to 'enjoy it' and not stress about getting pregnant. *Enjoy it!* Those were her words.

So after turning multiple shades of red, I say the worst thing one could possibly say: 'Nothing.'

'Nothing!' she gasps, clutching her chest dramatically. 'You are *planning*, aren't you?'

Since all I can manage is a nervous 'well ...', she explodes.

'Well? Mona! Ramit and you have been married for four years now. First he said he wanted to concentrate on his career. We didn't say anything. Then you left your job and we didn't want to put pressure on you. But beta, now you're thirty-one years old! Girls have a biological cycle, you know.'

I want to tell her that yes, I do know, I passed ninth-grade science, thank you very much. But she's Ramit's mother. I can't say that. I just sit there, twirling my dupatta around my finger anxiously. But, I think I kind of understand the type of pressure she feels, with the other relatives asking her when she's going to start her grandparent quota. And Mummy does have our best interest in mind.

I think she does. Maybe.

'You know,' she looks around the room, as if to ensure that no one is eavesdropping, 'Perhaps you should go see a doctor ...'

I twist my dupatta even tighter around my finger.

'You're both happy, aren't you?'

Not being able to produce a kid is clearly a mark of not being 'happy'. I want to say something, I really do, but being with Mummy is like being in the principal's office. Words bounce around in your brain and nothing appropriate ever makes it to the lips.

I can't get myself to say a single word. Finally, she pats my knee.

'*Ab kar lo, beta. Ab toh tumhara apna ghar bhi hai.*' Yes, like we hadn't been having sex because we were living in a rented flat!

Then follows the lecture that I dutifully nod along with, and as soon as it finishes, I run out at full speed. And promptly bump into the newly pregnant Mohini. She gives me a look of such sympathy that I feel like strangling her!

Ramit

Almost choked as Shaan, Swaroop, Abhiroop and a couple of their friends engulfed me at the airport. They took me directly to sheher to have some Babbu ka mutton tikka. We watched as Babbuji slashed open a 200gm pack of Amul butter and flung it on the sizzling pan. A bead of sweat dripped into it and only when that crackled did he know that the pan was hot enough for the mutton. Using a rusted knife, he hammered the chops and pushed them into the pool of darkening butter. Then he picked the dirtiest cloth available, used it to wipe a steel plate and plopped the cholesterol on it. I swallowed a rush of acid that rose to my mouth along with my pride. My cousins seemed unaffected, and I couldn't have them think I'd become a fussy dilliwala.

Smacked my fingers and made the appropriate appreciative noises, then got some packed for Mona for effect. The cousins clapped me on my back and we had decided the batting order for our gully cricket match before we even got home.

Mona

Yesterday, right before the sangeet, I had terrible acidity (bloody Babbu's mutton tikkas!) and spent the evening throwing up. I was totally offended at how much joy my sickness was giving people. I had just about returned from my first bout when an excited cousin, Suttu, went running to tell everyone I was throwing up. The room was suddenly flooded with thrilled-looking people. It broke up a game of cricket – that's how serious it was. Everyone asked me to lie down with my feet up and not take any medicines. I didn't get it at first. How naïve could I have been!

I had to throw up another couple of times before they let me have half a Digene. I think I heard some people congratulating Mummy as well. Ramit was as confused as I was. He was the only one who kept asking me what I'd eaten – everyone else sniggered at his question!

When Ramit and I were finally left alone, he asked me gently if I were sure I was not pregnant. I opened up my bag and thrust the half-empty pack of Whisper Ultra in his face. 'I'm currently using these. What do you think?'

I didn't care how awful I felt, I had to attend the bloody sangeet to make a point.

Ramit

Why can't Mummy have these embarrassing conversations with Mona instead of me? She insisted on sitting me down to talk about not letting Mona dance at the sangeet, since throwing up obviously meant that my wife was pregnant. I had to tell her all about the Whisper Ultra pack to finally get her to let me go. And then she muttered something about my lack of manners for discussing such private things with my mother.

Sex life, okay.

Menstruation, not.

So there we were. Mona insisted on dancing to all the Punjabi numbers so that all suspicion was thrown out of the window. And dragged me to the dance floor for company. The speakers were blaring '*Lak twenty-eight kudi da, forty-seven weight kudi da*'.

Mona snorted. 'Forty-seven weight. Here. In the land of pure ghee.'

Didn't want to say anything, but Mona hasn't ever been forty-seven kilos either, even if Dehradun doesn't have pure ghee.

'I feel like I'm at Prince Charming's ball,' Mona commented, shaking her head. 'Everyone here is wearing a gown! Including the duelling Daisy chachi and Nishi bua. All except Mummy in her starched sari and me, of course, in my outdated anarkali. Look, even Dadi's outfit looks like a gown!'

As I turned to look, Roshini, Abhiroop's wife, came charging at me, first tripping on whatever golden monstrosity she'd draped herself in, then balancing her squirmy two-year-old dangling from her hip, and said, 'Ramit bhaiya, now toh you should also have a baby. Little Roshan needs someone to play with.'

As if I'm responsible for her child's entertainment! I offered the kid my iPhone.

Mona

And right before leaving Amritsar, I celebrated my thirty-first birthday. In the midst of the Deol family.

The bheed stood around me as I blew the candles on the *Jams and Cakes* cake that Daisy chachi and Nishi bua both turned up their nose at.

Then some kind soul in the crowd pointed out that there were only thirty candles when I was actually turning thirty-one. Now, the one thing I do know is that the Deol family lacks mathematical genes, but trust them to emerge from the dark when it comes to my age. Before I could say anything, Mummy jumped in, saying I was thirty only. There were some murmurs of protest but no one messes with Mummy.

Right after the cake cutting, someone with their mouth full of pineapple cream cake, which, FYI, I hate – not the lack of manners, the flavour of cake – said, 'Bhabi, *is saal toh good news de hi do*!'

Ramit's ears turned pink.

And I got another taste of Babbu's mutton tikkas in my mouth.

Week LMP minus 3

If you aren't getting pregnant, just
keep trying

Mona

Such trying times.

Ramit returned to work with a vengeance – as if he'd been gone for months, when it was only a weekend. What does he do in that office, anyway? He's quite incapable of having an affair, that's for sure. He is the worst workaholic I've ever known. Even his mistress would leave him.

Two years ago when I'd quit my job to work on my own thing, everyone had naturally thought it was so I could concentrate on getting pregnant. 'Have a baby now that you're free!' Do people even know that your baby-maker needs to be 'free' too?

Ramit had scurried off and I was left to do all the packing by myself.

Mr Gopal, our landlord, asked both the Aggarwals on the first floor as well as us on the second to vacate by Monday. He claims his sons are returning to Delhi with their families and they wanted the two floors refurbished for them. I think it's a lie. I think he's finally caught on to how much rent he can actually be making in Green Park vs what we are paying him.

I was okay with it. We were planning to move next month anyway as our *very own house* was ready for possession. I only wished I had started packing much earlier instead of wasting all my time running around for Chiku's wedding to get my anarkalis altered.

The packing was too much for me to handle by myself so I had to phone Mom – my mom – and ask her to come down from Doon. Mom sent Shania instead, which was no help at all. All my sister did was chuck stuff into the carton saying, 'Di, do you really need this?' She thinks I'm a hoarder. And then she wanted to take a smoke break every half hour. I have a good mind to tell on her. She is getting skinnier by the minute and I wonder how she manages to go trekking and backpacking with the amount of damage she's done to her lungs.

She's into some sort of hippie thing, my twenty-eight-year-old sister Shania. She wears these gunji tops and tiny, torn shorts, and has a collection of wild headscarves, and smokes like a chimney, and wants to go trekking everywhere. But it's a phase. It's always a phase with her. She was all gypsy queen in college, wearing all sorts of cheap trinkets and sounding like a wind chime in long floral skirts and belly-dancing type of waistbands. And then she went through that horrid goth phase during my wedding, wearing black for all the ceremonies. People were freaking out about her being a witch. The camps and shorts and legs and cleavage have been around for a year now, and we're sure the next phase will hit us any day.

Earlier, I would regularly lecture her on getting a job and settling down, but she claims she has too much of the world to see before she can settle down. (Now who's being all Simran-like from *DDLJ*!) She returned from Goa last month with a horrid lizard tattoo that goes right up her thigh. It made Mom so mad, she called *me* up and yelled at *me* for not finding Shania a boy! If only she knew how many boys Shania has found for herself since she turned twelve. I blame it solely on Mom and Dad for not setting her right from the start. They spoilt it all by giving her an exotic name like Shania. I wish they'd saved some creativity for me. In school, college, post-grad, office, everywhere, I was forever Ajit's *Loin ki Mona, Mona ke saath Sona.* And have you noticed how some Punjabi aunties pronounce it? Moddha! DDH – as in the Hindi alphabet that no one can start a song with when you play antakshari and have to sing '*ddhing-ddhong-ddhing ek do teen…*'

Anyway, sometime during the packing, we started discussing the Amritsar trip. And I told her about Mohini being pregnant.

'*Ek aur pregnant? What does this Deol family eat?*'

'I'm quite sick of it all, vaise,' she continued. 'All my friends are getting married and having babies. I don't even want to log on to Facebook any more. *Ek toh,* what's the deal? Why do all babies look the same? Is it the same kid doing the rounds? It might as well be. Bhagwan just has a photocopy machine, I tell you.'

She looked at me for an answer – obviously, I had none. But I knew how she felt.

Earlier, it didn't bother me when my friends posted pictures of their newly made baby. I was at least ahead of the single ones, since I'd married young.

But at thirty plus, my friends were sending their kids to school! Or having more kids. Though, to be honest, there was not so much about seconds on Facebook because hey, they're seconds. It was routine. Even when people announce the arrival of their second one, it's not them who's to be congratulated. It's all about 'my first-born now has a baby brother/sister'. Rather mean to the second one, I think. I was glad I was the first-born in my family. Who would've boasted about a child like Shania, in any case?

'*Vaise*, di,' Shania said thoughtfully. 'In the movies, why do they say '*Main tumhare bachche ki maa banne wali hoon*'? Why doesn't the woman ever say *humare bachche ki*? Either she's saying it's all your fault I'm pregnant or it's all your responsibility now.'

I told her sternly to stop discussing pregnancies and get on with sorting out the bookshelf. As if I haven't been thinking about this stuff enough already!

I'd always been more concerned about Ramit's mother not having a grandchild. Ramit is, after all, her only child, her only hope. At least Mom has Shania. But just one look at her pierced tongue, her micro shorts, that lizard tattoo peeking out from those micro-shorts and her unending string of boyfriends, and I know I am most likely my mom's only hope too. Well, for a *legitimate* grandchild at least.

Ramit

Got home slightly late. Mona looked like she was going to explode. Don't know why. The whole point of Shania being there was so that she could help with the packing. Not me.

To make amends, I'd offered to book the movers and packers for the weekend. But apparently that was not good enough. Mona flung some fungus-infested canvas suitcase at me, asking me to pack up my own cupboard.

Wish I lived in the era of servile wives instead of henpecked husbands.

Mona

One thing I asked him to do and he has palmed it off! And guess who to? My very own traitor of a sister, who had been missing in action all week, meeting this gang and that, attending reunion pe reunion, taking cigarette break pe cigarette break. And then this morning, I actually found her sitting cross legged in front of his cupboard, folding up Ramit's shirts and trousers conscientiously. He, of course, had run out of the house on the pretext of some meeting.

He must have tipped her heavily.

Ramit

It cost me quite a bit, but I knew Shania would do a good job. Anyway, there were only a few shirts and trousers. How hard can that be? And some vests. And some socks. And some briefs.

Shit! The briefs!

Mona

I entered the room later to find Shania holding up Ramit's favourite Humpty Dumpty briefs. He's got them in five colours – yellow, red, blue, green and purple. And I don't mean nice pastels. They are as bright and sunny as it gets. With Humpty Dumpty's face right on the crotch.

In any other situation, I would have been embarrassed for him and whipped them off her hands, but this time, it served him right!

'Di!' she said, holding them up against her, her bratty grin plastered on her face. 'Is this what it is? You have a fetish for

Humpty Dumpty? I am your sexy, sexy lovah!' she started to sing.

I opened my mouth to tell her to shut up, but something else had already distracted her ... oh no.

Ramit

Shit! Shit! Shit! The Condoms!

Mona

'Chocolate-flavoured condoms? Ooh di! This is getting more and more interesting!'

And then, I swear, I saw her pocket two boxes.

I'm going to tell on her, you wait and see. My poor, innocent mother deserves to know what type of child she's raising. Raised. Raising. It's still not too late.

Ramit

Immediately called Shania and unhired her. She took away half a pack of very expensive cigars as a bribe for not mentioning the unmentionables found in my cupboard to anyone else.

Mona

The packers took sixteen hours to pack our stuff as opposed to the six they'd promised, and I was hopping mad.

I kept looking outside and noticing the efficiency of the packers the Aggarwals had hired, and was pleased to see their progress was even slower than ours. Mrs Aggarwal was throwing a fit and her brat was not helping the process either – he kept wailing about how they were packing off his tricycle and hitting his haggard-looking mother. Why do children hit their parents? My child would never hit me! He'd be meek and do as he was told. He'd sit in the corner and colour and read books and generally be calm and quiet, like his father.

Talking of who, Ramit had planned to run off to another 'one hour only' meeting in the afternoon, but I had a major showdown with him, post which he quickly cancelled the appointment and was spending the day supervising the packers.

Shania was unperturbed by my turning into a raging dragon and coolly insisted on being dropped off to the airport. Yes, in the middle of all the chaos! I told her to cab it, but she wailed about how broke she was and how unsafe cabs were and how she didn't understand Delhi. So, I had to drive off to the airport so that madam could catch her flight to Puducherry. She seemed to have found an ashram there and is going to stay there for a week. Goodbye hiking phase, I thought.

When I returned, Ramit was already getting the truck loaded. I was so impressed that I looked around in amazement for a few minutes. And then realized that something was amiss. Our thirty-two-inch TV had turned into a forty-one-inch one and there was a rather dirty green tricycle huddled next to it. That's when I realized that Ramit was helping Mrs Aggarwal pack.

He and I are no longer on speaking terms.

Week LMP minus 2

In their thirties, women have about a 15 per cent chance
of getting pregnant in any single ovulation cycle

Mona

You may now officially call me Super Woman! I am capable of doing anything and everything! With the exception of remembering my ovulation dates, but that's a separate issue.

We are all moved in and set up. All thanks to me! Fine – Ramit had a small role to play in getting the telephone and satellite dish installed on Sunday, but other than that, I did everything. I got the drawing room set up, the bedroom done, the guest room done, all our clothes put in the closets and even the linen in the linen cupboards. And we *have* a linen cupboard! Huge achievement compared to stashing them into the side table drawers, which would then not shut, in our previous house.

But what I was most proud of myself for was having found a maid! Lakshmi is punctual, clean, well-networked and hasn't stolen anything in three days.

I also managed to go for a walk around the colony today, after working non-stop for five days on getting the house in order, and I think it was a brilliant investment!

Now we are no longer Delhites. We are Gurgaonvaasis. Okay, Gurugramvaasis.

We've moved into this newly constructed gated colony that comprises only villas – built in pairs – with a white picket fence as a boundary around each, complete with individual gardens and driveways. We've never had assigned parking before. In Green Park, there were times when we wished we could park our cars one on top of the other, and almost did. This is a complete luxury!

On the other side, and in front of the villas, is a lane separating the next pair of villas, and there is a common park a couple of lanes away that has a jogging track, a basketball area, a sand pit (my kids will have a blast growing up here!) and swings. And there are little patches of carnations everywhere. Which is very cool, because we're called Carnation Estate. And I have a patch of pink roses and a papaya tree in the garden. It's just too exciting!

The first lot of houses were ready for possession last year, so the colony's already half full, including our twin villa. Our neighbours have been here for the last six months, I'm told, but I'm yet to catch sight of them. They paid extra to get possession earlier and, judging by the size of the cars standing outside with the uniformed chauffeurs, I don't find that hard to believe. I've also seen a host of servants running around.

But whatever, all-in-all, I'm so happy we're settled in! Ramit's office is close by (not very close, but it's in Gurgaon) and we have a fantastic new house. I can now finally start working on losing weight, work on my business idea and get on with some family planning!

Ramit

I'm a little worried Shania has left behind some of her 'things' and Mona has decided to try them or something. Because every day when I return from work, she's almost high on energy and bursting with enthusiasm, showing me some new fixture around the kitchen or going on about a new curio in the living room or shoving curtain designs down my throat.

Today it was something to do with a name plate. Whether it should be black against white or white against black. I wanted to tell her to speak to my cousin Suttu, since she's studying design, but I'm not sure it would've gone down too well. I've learnt not to mention the bheed on our time off.

Mona

Picked up the nameplate and sent a picture of it to Ramit. His response? K.

Ekta Kapoor would love him. She's the only other person I know who needs to deal with as many K's as I do.

Anyway, I thought it looked nice. I walked out, hung it neatly on our little gate, and stepped back to admire it – DEOLS, VILLA NO. 22. And then I happened to look across to our neighbour's. It said LAILA AND SHASHI, COTTAGE 23, CARNATION ESTATE.

Cottage? Excuse me? Does our sales deed not say 'villa'? (Okay, maybe it says house number, but the builders always say villa!) So who are they to call it a cottage?

Now I'm a little embarrassed that I've got a wannabe 'villa' written on my nameplate. Cottage sounds so much better.

Took a walk around the colony. Stomped around, to be precise. There are two more people who have 'villa no.' mentioned under their names. None have a stupid 'cottage' written under theirs.

But most people just have the house number. They're so uncool.

Ramit

Got home to find Mona sulking on the couch. Wondered if yet another relative had been knocked up. But she was on some tangential I'm-losing-my-identity trip.

Finally figured it had something to do with the damn nameplate. She's extremely upset about being labelled a Deol. I don't blame her.

She wants to put both our names on it. And add Carnation Estate. Don't know how that'll help because the entire area is Carnation Estate, but she insists it's important if a letter comes her way. I don't remember the last time we received a letter. Even wedding invites are sent via email now. She plans to get a matching letterbox installed outside.

Mona

I know I should be asleep but, seriously, what kind of a name is *Laila*? So MTV! That is surely not her *real* name.

I'm not keen to meet the neighbours at all. Flashy cars, flashy names, flashy nameplates. They've totally spoilt my neighbourhood.

Ramit

Text from Mona: *Come home early*

    Replied: *K*

    Text from Mona: *By 7*

    Replied: *K*

    Text from Mona: *You're just saying that. You won't come by even 9, will you?*

    Replied: *Will do*

    Text from Mona: *Is that a will do by 7 or will do by 9?*

    Replied: *9*

    Text from Mona: *Are you in a meeting?*

    Replied: *No*

    Text from Mona: *Then why are you sending me single-word messages?*

    Replied: *Be home by 9. Love you.*

That should settle it. I hope it's not another nameplate.

Mona

Okay, then. I've got the house in order and have decided that this weekend is the one!

It's our brand new house and we will inaugurate it with a brand new baby. I am, of course, being overly ambitious. I've had the same hopes before every ovulation cycle the past twelve months. And to make matters worse, I keep forgetting my dates.

When we first started trying a year ago, we thought – do the deed, sow the seed. With no contraceptive, we thought we'd make a baby immediately. Nothing happened.

In the second month, I went off caffeine and papaya and refused to lift heavy things because, you know, best to be careful. But then again, nothing. Which was okay. Maybe we were just new to *not* using protection.

Month three: I Googled the most 'dangerous' dates in one's cycle. And for the first time, I kept a record of my dates. That's how prepared I was!

Month four: I went lingerie shopping. Out of jockeys. Into La Senza. After a highly uncomfortable month of synthetic, itchy underwear, nothing. Threw away the La Senza.

Month five: I forced myself to feel queasy every morning. Really believed in it. Nothing.

Anyway, thirteen months later, I've realized you can't snap your fingers and say, 'I want a baby' and just have it. One has to be patient.

But still, this weekend is going to be it! After all, we're in our own house, like Mummy says.

Ramit

Mona's saying there's lasagne and cheesecake for dinner. Her mother is a great cook and I'm so glad Mona has inherited her talent. My mother, on the other hand, has a house full of cooks, thank God.

At 7.00 Mona sent me a picture of herself. Haven't wrapped up work quicker.

Mona

The evening was officially ruined.

I made all of Ramit's favourite food, arranged a candlelight dinner, put up our brand new, posh-looking nameplate at the gate with our letterbox (MONA AND RAMIT DEOL, VILLA NO. 22 – did not stoop to the neighbour's wannabe level and use 'cottage'), dressed up in a short red dress, ironed my long hair – it's reaching my knees now – and put on some make-up. Then I pouted and took a selfie for Ramit. Ugh! Tried again – put a hand on one hip and clicked another one. Ended up looking like one of those women from the Moov ads. Deleted. Then took a full-length selfie in the mirror. Cursed myself for not choosing one of those slimming mirrors when we were doing up the house. Also wished the mirror would make me look taller. Then accidentally dropped the phone and when I reached to pick it up, it accidentally shot a picture of my cleavage and randomly sent it to Ramit. Well, at least it wasn't to the family group. Immediately got a text from Ramit saying he'd left office.

And then Mummy called from Amritsar. One of her staff teacher's daughter, who is thirty-seven, went in for IVF and is now pregnant.

Mummy spoke in hushed whispers and told me to 'relax', and next month she would find out more about IVF.

I was so stressed by the end of that conversation that when Ramit came to bed, I clamped up and feigned sleep. I did not want Mummy picturing me 'relaxing'!

Week LMP minus 1

Body fat may affect fertility

Ramit

Spotted a rather hot neighbour today. In really tiny shorts. Mona didn't see her. Hope she didn't see me looking at her either.

I wonder if I should tell Mona that she needs to lose some weight. She has been gaining some around her midriff. She is still, of course, one of the skinniest people in Punjab. But I worry about her. She just kind of lounges around in her trackpants all day.

She may want to join the gym.

Found her beaming at me when I joined her at the breakfast table.

'I'm 64.2 kilos today. 800gms down from Chiku's wedding. Thanks to your Babbu's mutton tikkas and the awful acidity. I should've just checked my weight a little earlier. Maybe I've actually lost a lot more.'

And then she reached for the toast and applied generous amounts of Nutella to it.

Mona

I quite like our living room.

I've placed this massive lamp from the Amritsar house near the window and kept Ramit's easy chair right next to it. It makes for a great reading spot. Especially since we've got a little bookshelf on the wall with all these leather-bound books stacked up in it. It's some sort of National Geographic series, which Ramit was into during his schooldays. I don't think he's ever gone through all of them. But anyway, it looks pretty classy in our living room.

I'm waiting for Ramit to return from office. He's just texted me to say he's leaving office and it's only 7.00 p.m.! Maybe it's baby-making night? I'll just ignore all calls from Mummy. And Mom.

Anyway, back to the living room. I'm sitting in his easy chair leafing through the *Femina* I bought, calculating my body mass index as the magazine suggests, sipping cardamom tea and eating some herby crackers – when the lights go on in our neighbours' home.

I can see right into their living room. Into their 'cottage', excuse me! It's a very pretty house, I have to admit. Golden and coral walls, white sofas. (White sofas are very daring. We had white sofas once in our Dehradun house till Jahangir, our dog, left paw marks all over it. Mom was livid!) They have some very nice lights. Very fancy lampshades. We'd seen these when we'd gone light shopping and these were definitely in the top range. They also have a fireplace (How firang!) and little mantle curios. Can't make out much of what the curios are like from this distance, but going by the rest of the house, must be expensive. There's a bright painting hanging above their sofa. Very artistic. I wish I could see what sort of carpet they have. We need a rug for our living room too. And now that I've seen that painting, maybe I should get one myself.

Then I see this tall, well-built man with salt-and-pepper hair, dressed in a grey shirt and black trousers, saunter into the room with a glass of, maybe, scotch. Obviously can't actually see that, but he looks like someone who'd drink scotch. He picks up a cigar and turns towards the door. Then this tall lady walks in. Can't see her face – she has her back towards me. She is very slim, has straight hair, and is wearing a well-fitted navy-blue dress. I'm guessing that is Laila of nameplate fame.

And then without any warning, they kiss. A long, passionate kiss. I turn away in embarrassment but then curiosity gets the better of me … they're kissing some more and … he is unbuttoning her dress!

I run up to my room, two stairs at a time, but not before turning off my own lamp in embarrassment.

Ramit

Yes, I know we need curtains and all that, but to go stomping away on a shopping spree the one day I get home on time is uncalled for.

Thankfully, Mona was at her efficient best and we were back with rather dark, thick curtains despite my argument against them. I was made to stand on the ladder till midnight to have them up in our living room. I joked about them being wasted in the living room because that's not where we needed our privacy – she didn't find that funny.

A lot of stomping this evening.
And no sex.

Mona

Unbuttoning her dress in the middle of the day! Evening! Whatever! Surely their staff could've walked in on them! I don't even let Lakshmi into our bedroom!

I eventually told Ramit about our X-rated neighbours but he just snickered.

And despite my story about how uncouth they are, Ramit decided to strike up a conversation with them when we were sitting out in the garden today! I didn't even want to look at them (how embarrassing to see someone you've seen naked … almost …) but Ramit called out to me and I had no choice.

My heart skipped a beat when I saw the tall man's face. I swear that for a second, I thought he was Milind Soman.

'Mona, this is Shashi Sachdev,' Ramit introduced me. I think he was a little louder than usual to ensure that I shut my gaping mouth. I tried my best to smile politely and not ogle at the man. But really, he's like some Greek god, with those chiselled features and dark skin and shapely lips…

'Hi Mona, nice to meet you,' he said, in a deep baritone that made me want to melt. He then turned to the woman beside to him. 'This is Laila.'

I turned to the well-manicured hand with bright red nailpolish reaching across the fence for my hand. I reluctantly had to take my hand out of my pockets and cursed myself for not putting cream this morning as I extended my scaly skin. She looked like a diva, a sexy supermodel.

She was as tall as him, or was wearing high heels to match his height – I couldn't see – and her ivory, smooth skin had probably never seen the onset of teenage acne. She had straight white teeth and voluptuous red lips, immaculately applied mascara around her sparkly hazel eyes, and straight brown-ish hair right out of shampoo ads.

I think I gaped at her in amazement, too. I am a bloody embarrassment!

She could be a foreigner. And they say they've moved from Singapore, so ...

'Hi Mona,' she said in this throaty, sexy voice – I think it's the cigarettes. She looks the sort. 'Welcome to the neighbourhood.'

I stood there silently as Ramit made small talk, trying not to feel like a colourless mouse.

And they both looked so fit. Shashi was in this half-sleeved shirt, and his biceps were so defined! My poor Ramit looked malnourished in comparison. I've decided to wake up early tomorrow onwards and give him freshly squeezed orange juice. The Amristari relatives are right: Ramit really is *kamzor*. He's got a lanky frame, bespectacled eyes, moppy hair – he is the stereotypical software engineer.

And then there was this goddess of a Barbie doll standing in front of me. Not a size zero, but with fat where it counts. I was in jeans and a loose T-shirt while her tiny waist was dressed in white trousers (Who is she? Jeetendra?) and a well-fitted baby-pink shirt. She'd rolled up her sleeves to flaunt a rather expensive looking watch (who wears watches nowadays! Even if it is a Rolex) and she had solitaires on her earlobes. They looked very hip.

She was also wearing the most massive solitaire ring. I felt like kicking myself for leaving my wedding ring upstairs. It may not be a massive solitaire but it has sixteen diamonds. Mummy had told me this proudly when she had shoved it up my fat finger, as is tradition, at the shagan ceremony. That's right. Ramit didn't even give me a ring. It was Mummy.

I don't even want to think of the impression I've made on them. Ramit at least was wearing a branded Nike sweatshirt.

Ramit kept ooh-aahing about some Jonas League firm Milind-Shashi works for. I nodded along knowledgably and tried to match Ramit's impressed expression, but I don't know what the hell Jonas League is. Though I did gather he's a lawyer.

'I was with their Singapore office earlier,' Shashi said in a deep voice. 'We just moved here six months ago.' He had a slight twang to his accent. I didn't think people from Singapore would have an accent.

'We moved here so that Laila's office could be close by. She heads marketing for Sparq.'

I tried not to gasp. Sparq is the top cosmetics brand in the country! In the world! They make the coolest ads and were rated one of the best companies to work for in the country. If she is head of marketing, she must be at least forty years old. I am very quick at calculating people's age. She certainly doesn't look her age. But all that mascara and lipstick made sense now. They're all Sparq products. I'm sure she was wearing foundation too. No one's skin can be that perfect.

But just look at them showing off! Telling us she 'heads' marketing rather than works in marketing and that they've just come in from Singapore. I don't like them one bit, if you ask me. Not one bit!

'What about you, Mona? Are you working somewhere?'

Ramit

The dreaded question.

'Uh … no … I'm on a break,' I heard Mona stutter.

She hates being asked about her work. I keep telling her it's only a matter of time before she starts her business and really, it's all her choice, but …

'Well, it's good to finally have some neighbours,' Laila said. 'We should have you guys over sometime for a drink.'

I saw Mona nodding rather vigorously. 'Yes, that sounds wonderful. In fact, we're just setting up the bar at our place too so we must have you guys over once we're done,' she says.

Impressive. Mona had never mentioned setting up a bar before.

Mona

I swear Laila shot me a quick glance to see if I'm too *behenji* to drink. I'm avoiding Ramit's eye after the bar comment. Now we're getting one, whether I like it or not! We'll just move that damned Amritsar lamp out of the way.

'Great! Sometime during the week then,' Laila said flashing another one of her dazzling smiles. Surely this perfect set of teeth can't be real! I hear even top Indian actresses need to get their teeth fixed.

We exchanged some more small talk before parting ways and they walked off to their Mercedes, hand in hand. I quickly latched on to Ramit's arm as we walked back to our plastic Neelkamal garden chairs.

'Jonas League!' Ramit sounded thoroughly impressed. 'That's the biggest law firm ever! And she works at Sparq. She can get you some free products.'

I didn't speak to Ramit for an hour after that. I can't believe he thinks I need beauty products!

I don't think he noticed me sulking, though. He was too engrossed in his phone.

No wonder we're not making any babies.

Week LMP

Your pregnancy journey begins

Mona

The chums are back. Another month of not being pregnant.

I told Ramit and he gave me a hug. I don't even know why I'm depressed. It's probably because I feel like I'm letting everyone down. I've ignored all calls from Mom and Mummy today.

In the evening, I realized they can't possibly know my period dates and I'm being overly paranoid. Hell, I have a tough time remembering my own dates. So I decided to call them back.

'*Kuch hua*?' my mom asked me the minute she answered the phone.

'What do you mean!'

I was aghast! How was she keeping track of my dates better than me! I have the most interfering family ever! At least my mum-in-law would never keep track of my dates. My own mum's really becoming too much!

Like how she keeps saying that so-and-so is not having a baby cause she's so busy with her career. So much stress. What's the obsession with money? Is her husband not earning enough? She should concentrate on the family.

And the other so-and-so who's not having a baby – it's her lack of career to blame. She toh is a housewife. Left her job to become pregnant *lekin ho nahin raha*. It's like being constipated despite having Isabgol.

So annoying! I had a good mind to slam down the phone.

'Shania *ke ticket ka ... kuch hua*?' She continued, 'Shania's stuck in that dreadful Puducherry, na. She's been telling us to help her with the tickets na. That's why I'd messaged you in the morning to ask Ramit's office or someone else to help with it. *Kuch hua ki nahin*?'

I think I'm a bunch of nerves about this whole pregnancy thing. My poor mother ...

We made small talk, discussed Mom's fear of Shania returning with another tattoo, didn't discuss babies and all-in-all, it was a good conversation. I put the phone down and called back Mummy.

'It's been one month since Chiku's wedding,' she said immediately.

My heart was thumping. She remembers I was chumming at Chiku's wedding. It's been a month. She's the one who's been calculating. I braced myself for the interrogation.

'I miss you both,' she said longingly. 'It's been so long since I last saw you!'

Oh! I really am getting too paranoid.

'We were just there, Mummy,' I told her gently.

'But that was all so hectic. I hardly got to spend any time with you. Especially with Daisy going berserk.'

'Did Nishi bua really do it on purpose then?'

Mummy lowered her voice. 'It was Nayantara only who leaked the design.'

I gasped. That's Daisy chachi's very own daughter-in-law. This was big gossip indeed!

'Yes. Imagine that! I think she was peeved with Daisy because Daisy threw that chaat party last summer on the same day Nayantara's mother had her high-tea party.' High tea? Is this seriously Amritsar we're talking about? 'So anyway, I asked Nishi finally and she told me Nayantara had sent her details of the design.'

'Daisy chachi will get a full-on shock if she finds out.'

'Hmm. Nayantara and the kids are coming to Delhi next to next week. Her brother's there, na. She said this time she'll definitely call you.'

Oh no.

Oh no, oh no, oh no, oh no, oh no …

'In fact, Mona …'

No, no, no, no, no …

'Why don't you call all the cousins over for dinner?'

NO!

'There are so many of them there. It will be a nice reunion.'

We just had a reunion at Chiku's wedding! No!

'Now that we have a nice house …' she went on.

We don't have a house! Ramit and I have a house!

'You should have lots of parties before you get busy with starting a family.'

Starting a family! Because, of course, Ramit and I aren't a family. A 'family' is incomplete unless you've been through sleepless nights together with a bawling kid. I am fuming again.

'Ramit is busy with work, Mummy. I'll ask him and figure out a date,' I said dismissively, hoping she'd get the hint.

'Ramit is always busy with work,' Mummy brushed me aside. 'He needs to get busy with other things.'

And then it happened.

'It's been a month since you had your period here. Have you had it again this month?'

Ramit

When I got into bed, Mona told me, 'I'm really quite tired of all this interference, Ramit!'

I know how she feels. But it's also an opportunity to, you know ... I reached out for her hand and gave it a sympathetic squeeze. 'Then let's make a baby.' I knew I was grinning, despite trying to look nonchalant.

'I'm chumming!' she growled.

She is perpetually chumming!

I didn't realize I said that out loud. Damn! After that, she bit my head off!

I thought you're supposed to PMS before the period rather than during it.

Anyway, I decided to be all manly and tell her not to get so worked up about the whole thing. I told her she shouldn't get stressed because she doesn't even like children to begin with.

She chewed up the whatever was left of me after that. I swear I saw fangs.

I finally decided to give her a tight hug instead of saying any more stupid things.

Mona

Ramit snuggled up next to me. He put away his laptop. He put away his phone.

Wow! The one time my husband shows me affection, I'm chumming.

Ramit

So I'm in office today – unshaven. People think someone has died. The real reason is that we have run out of shaving cream.

Mona's bought a year's supply of sanitary napkins! There was an avalanche when I opened the utility cupboard that Mona has so proudly allotted to our toiletries, looking for some shaving cream.

She obviously has no hope in hell about getting pregnant. She kept saying I should be proud of her for saving me some money by buying these things on one of these online grocery websites. She really needs a new hobby.

Mona

I've made up my mind. It's not about getting pregnant. It's about doing something in life!

Of course I have my business idea to chalk out, but first, I need to lose weight like that stupid Laila-Majnu woman next door. You can't even sit with your curtains open now without seeing her flit in and out of her house looking like a super model.

So I got off my expanding butt and went for a walk to the park. Met a Mrs Kapoor. When people introduce themselves as Mrs So-and-so, I'm compelled to respond with a Mrs too. So I told her I'm Mrs Deol. And then the customary question – am I related to Sunny Deol?

Mummy says that if Ramit hadn't married me, they would have gotten him hitched to their neighbour Babita, aka, Bobby. Can you imagine that?

* * *

Why didn't I ask Mrs Kapoor if she was related to Raj Kapoor, Rishi Kapoor, Ranbir Kapoor? Why do these smart alec comebacks only come to me in the middle of the night?

* * *

Also, which thirty-year-old calls herself 'Mrs So-and-so'? Mrs Kapoor is possibly just as old as me, with a six-year-old who was quite bratty at the park. The child was unimaginatively called Asha. Mrs Kapoor's first name must be even more unimaginative.

When I have kids, I'll make sure I spend hours researching their names and find a name no one else has!

Like Nadia. I've always loved the name Nadia. Like the gymnast?

* * *

Who am I kidding! How will I ever produce a child if all this man has accomplished by 2.00 a.m. is an even more densely populated 'SENT' folder?

Week 2

Your fertile window is approaching

Ramit

Why did we even bother with windows in our living room? Mona has made an unspoken rule of pulling close the curtains in the living room all day.

She reasons that it's even more embarrassing now that we now know their names and exactly how they look.

Mona

We're really turning into social hermits. A lot of our friends now have babies and we don't want to be around any wailing children on our evenings off. Especially because that stupid question almost always comes up.

'Arrey, Mona. You've been married four years, no! What plans?'

And then comes the dilemma of what to tell your friends should you tell them the truth – that you're trying but unable to conceive? Will they give you some good advice or will they look at you sympathetically, the way your family does? Or should you just play it cool, so that when you do conceive you can use the 'it was an accident' line.

So we're avoiding just about everyone now.

Except our supermodel neighbours. They've invited us over for dinner. And not just us, they said they're having a few friends over too.

I've spent most of Friday peering out of my window. God! I'm turning into one of those nosey aunties.

I've seen their help scuttling around. A lot of trips are being made to the market and I see crates of soft drinks and alcohol being wheeled out. Dammit! I can't drink. I'm trying to have a baby! But if I don't drink, Laila Sachdev will think I'm all *behenji*. I text Ramit, asking him what we should do about the situation. There is, of course, no response.

I think we've also been lied to. It's not just a few friends who've been invited – going by the arrangements, it's clearly a large party! What if I wasn't Laila Sachdev's neighbour? I would have never known the scale of this party and ended up going in my jeans.

Lakshmi, my cook, decided to join in on my snooping. I was rather indignant at being caught in the act, so I turned back to my book while she continued to look on.

'Very rich!' she sighed, and then proceeded to tell me that they do generally throw such lavish parties. Lots of guests. Lots of celebrations. In fact, last time they had called Lakshmi too. At this point I looked at Lakshmi suspiciously. So she hastily clarified – she hadn't been invited as a guest but only to help with the chapatis.

I feigned disinterest but she went on. She said they have plenty of staff. Leela, Laila's first lady. Leela's husband, their household manager. Two chauffeurs. One cleaning lady. I was rather alarmed at the number of staff they had employed for just the two of them but then I saw that Lakshmi was only making a point of how much work she was doing single-handedly for us and how ingratiated we should feel. Which is rubbish. Her cooking is significantly below average.

I'm glad to be escaping her cooking today. Laila has obviously hired caterers.

Cooking stations were being set up at the back and a team of caterers and uniformed waiters were lining up.

Once Lakshmi left and the evening streetlights came on, I returned to my vigil and watched as Laila's BMW pulled into the driveway.

Her staff is really, really good. Very fancy. Her uniformed chauffeur rushed out to open the door and she strode into the house, talking on her phone. She was dressed in a grey trouser suit and I dropped the idea of fitting into my own trouser suit for tonight's party. It's very wannabe for a non-working woman to turn up in office clothes for a dinner. I needed to find a dress!

Five minutes later Laila was in the garden, inspecting the fairylights draping her fence and the little angeethis placed close to each cluster of chairs. Someone rushed towards her, holding a tray of snacks. She tasted them all and gave some instructions to the chef. She even checked the linen on all the tables. Then, she pointed to the corner of the garden, to where they brought out a large table and started setting up the bar.

I'm totally nervous about this dinner now. I better find a dress I can still fit into.

Ramit

Wow! What an evening it turned out to be!

Got home to find Mona in a tiny black dress. It was a good change from seeing her in her regular tracks and tees, and she was wearing lipstick and perfume and these nice little earrings, and her hair was pinned up. I debated whether we should have our own little private party and forget the neighbours but she seemed to be on a mission to not let Laila think we were uncool, so we decided to go after all. I had to shower and shave and change into something decent.

It was actually quite nice – great ambience, good music, smooth alcohol – and I met a lot of potential clients, including the head of sales of my previous organisation. He was interested to know what I was doing, and later, more people joined in the conversation, so now I have a couple of meetings lined up for next week.

I was a little worried that me talking shop would bore Mona, but she seemed to have found company too. And she really was enjoying her wine.

Mona

Woohoo! We seemed to be at some sort of Page Three party! The people were so good-looking, I felt like I was in a magazine for the rich and famous. I think I spotted a TV celebrity.

Milind-Shashi was sashaying around with his baritone laughter and Laila Sachdev was playing gracious hostess in a tiny, off-shoulder pink dress that looked like it could malfunction any minute. She even came and chatted with me for a while, and then put an arm around my waist and led me to a group of two-dimensional ladies.

I completely pigged out on the starters. Fried mozzarella, chicken quiche, prawn tempura and what not! Two wines down, I even started contributing to the conversation.

'You've moved in recently?' one of the women, someone called Tina Tej Mushran, asked me. 'It seems to be a lovely neighbourhood! I was a little doubtful why Laila would pick something so far from the main hustle-bustle, and also, these builders are new, aren't they? But when we came over last time, we were absolutely floored. Plus, it's Laila, you know? She can make anything beautiful. I guess that's why she's in the beauty business. And her parties are always so grand. I mean, today, she said it's a small dinner for close friends. But look at the scale! I wonder who the caterers are? These snacks are delicious! Anyway, honey, tell me about you! What do you do?'

'Well, I'm currently on a break. I was with a travel company.' No point telling her that was two years ago. 'Now I'm just, you know, settling in.'

'And your husband, Ramit? Just the two of you, then?'

'Yes, just the two of us. What about you?'

'Tej and I have been married eight years now. Three little ones.'

She had that perfect figure *after* three children. Hell, I was wearing my tummy tucker.

'In fact, Sameer, my youngest, turns two months old this weekend!'

I almost choked on my wine. Perfect figure after *two* months!

'How long have you and your husband been married?' she asked me.

'Four years …'

'Oh. Not planning kids any time soon?'

I hate making small talk.

Oh well, at least the wine was good!

Ramit returned after a while and I was clinging to him for the rest of the evening to show that we're indeed 'happy', even if we have no child to show for it. Ramit was a little confused at my public show of affection but played along in any case, holding my hand tightly.

Ramit

Mona was swaying. Had to hold her hand all evening. She couldn't stand straight.

But drunk Mona is a lot of fun ... for others. She cracked jokes and made lots of conversation with strangers and was overall quite a hit at the party.

The goodbye hugs were never-ending. You'd never believe she was meeting these people for the first time.

Mona

The wine was yum yum yum yum!

Ramit looked yum yum yum yum!

Ramit

Woke up with a hysterical call from the mother-in-law. Apparently my sister-in-law has scurried off to Pune to some other ashram now. Since Mona is still hungover, I was given the task of talking Shania out of it.

Called her and don't know how but got conned into transferring her 25K.

Week 3

Your baby has been conceived

Mona

Mom called. No talk about Shania's sudden flight to Pune and her newfound obsession with spirituality. I got an alert that my credit card had been swiped at a sari house in Pune. Changed my passcode immediately. Don't know when I'd shared it with her in the first place.

Anyway, Mom was on a different tangent. Her friend's daughter, who went to school with me, is now expecting her second child. Mom also subtly mentioned that Ramit and I should take a holiday and that we needed to de-stress. And then she not so subtly spoke about my cousin Aarti having an IVF and said, 'There's no shame in it anymore'. Which is a lie because last year when my friend got it done, Mom made a big deal about it!

But seriously, clearly nothing is working out. We might as well face it. We have conception issues. I only wonder if it's me or Ramit. If it's Ramit, a Deol, it would be quite the shocker.

So I did the unspeakable. I Googled 'How to have a baby'.

There are apparently positions one needs to adopt. Positions! Including how to have a girl and how to have a boy. What is the world coming to?

It said you should place a cushion under your bum to better your chances at conceiving. I exited the website immediately.

The website also says you need to do it every two to three days. Considering how Ramit stays glued to his phone, we can only have phone sex at that frequency!

Anyway, I deleted all my browsing history.

Ramit

What is with Mona? She gets jumpy every time I touch her phone.

Wonder whose messages she's hiding. She did have a ball of a time at the party and I've seen her looking out of our window at Shashi Sachdev's house often enough.

Maybe I should spend less time at the office.

Mona

So much for that. Now that *I* feel comfortable leaving the curtains of the living room open, Ramit has started closing them.

Anyway, I have started going for a walk around the park regularly. Well, at least I went again this week. The same park where 'Mrs Kapoor' comes with little Asha. And guess who I saw today, jogging around in the tiniest of shorts! Laila Sachdev. Shorts! In December!

She immediately walked over to say hello. I could almost hear Mrs Kapoor's radar beeping.

Laila mainly made small talk about the weather. She could've fooled me about being affected by it, given the length of her shorts! I politely asked her how come she was running around the park at 4.00 p.m. Apparently, some year-end leaves pending so she's taken a week off. And they're off to Hong Kong for New Year's Eve.

She also told me she typically jogs in the morning, before leaving for work, but since she's on holiday now, she thought she'd go for a round in the evening.

Then said her friend Tina, who I had apparently 'hit it off with' the evening of the party, had taken my number and wanted to invite me for her Christmas party. I could feel Mrs Kapoor's watchful eyes on me. Anyway, I'm not sure I want to be associated with Laila Sachdev and her friends, who're too posh for my liking. I made some excuse about probably having plans or something and exited the conversation. She waved me goodbye and ran off. I continued with my 'brisk walk' around the park. It lasted fifteen minutes.

Mrs Kapoor caught up with me and breathlessly enquired about who the woman I had been talking to was. Clearly she isn't as clued into the colony as she pretends to be.

Ramit

Got hold of Mona's phone. No incriminating messages. But she's deleted her browsing history. That must mean something.

That Shashi Sachdev, she keeps comparing him to Milind Soman. And that's definitely not an insult, is it?

She's been so distracted lately.

Have taken two days off work. Can't have my wife having an affair.

Mona

Ramit and I are going away for the weekend! Yay! Take that, Laila I'm-so-cool-I'm-off-to-Hong-Kong Sachdev! We're as cool as you!

Okay, so we're not jet-setting to Hong Kong or wherever, but we're still going to Neemrana for the weekend and we will be staying in the suite! Not in the 3000-rupee room like we did last time.

I'm just too excited and hope I don't start chumming. That'll be a real bummer. I've forgotten the date again but it's probably supposed to be around now. Or next week. Or next to next. Dammit! I need to get myself a table calendar. A bedside table calendar. Or I should just ask Mummy or Mom – they are probably keeping track of my dates anyway.

Ramit

It's turning out to be a pretty good holiday. Mona and I got a chance to discuss this baby thing, and she confessed that she'd been jumpy because she'd Googled how to have a baby, and then deleted her browser history because she was embarrassed or something.

I didn't tell her I'd been snooping on her phone. Men don't snoop. Or at least, own up to snooping. Anyway, now I don't have to take holidays to get my wife away from good-looking neighbours. Looks like she's still interested in having a baby with me only.

Then we discussed IVF. Later, I spent a good hour reading up on it while she slept. It sounds pretty scary. And more importantly, it sounds very expensive. We've just bought a house. We can't afford IVF.

I think that basically does it.

We can't afford to have a baby.

* * *

But if that's what will make her happy, I'll ask Surjit about withdrawing my capital from the business for a while. That should help.

* * *

I really love Mona, you know. She's such a wonderful human being. She's so caring and pretty and…

Mona

Woke up to find Ramit cooing to my face. Buried my head in the pillow and slept again. We spent the whole day talking, and then he decided to turn to his phone. And now he finds time to coo?

What a waste of a holiday!

Week 4

Be patient while you wait

Mona

Lakshmi, the cook, came looking rather thrilled today. I asked her why. She said because of the pregnancy. I almost fainted.

She must be at least fifty! And didn't she have a twenty-five-year-old married daughter?

Then she clarified it's her daughter who's pregnant. This is her fourth child. They're trying for a boy this time.

And after that, as I sat in my living room, this flash of an idea came zipping into my head.

Ramit

Mona's lost it. Got a text from her. She suggests we adopt Lakshmi's grandchild if it's a girl and if she doesn't want it.

This baby business is driving her berserk.

Mona

I didn't get a K to that message from Ramit. I didn't get a response at all, really. But then I got a call from my friend Shubhra. She's expecting.

73

Then Shania called to tell me her friend Rustam's wife is expecting.

I needed a break. So I went out for a walk and looked for the colony dog to give a biscuit to. I hadn't realized till today that it was a she. And she looks ready to pop too.

That's five people I know who're expecting! Shubhra, Rustam's wife, just-back-from-honeymoon cousin Mohini, Lakshmi's daughter, and now the dog.

And all I get are questions.

Koi good news?

So pissed off!

Ramit

Mummy called. Said I have to call the bheed over and show them the new house. This is the least I can do for refusing to have the havan Dadi had insisted on. I couldn't hear her go on about that one again, so in irritation, immediately texted on the cousins' WhatsApp group, inviting them for dinner on Friday. Realized I hadn't bothered checking with the wife.

Mona's vocabulary blossoms in a 'Deol' situation.

Mona

What the hell was he thinking, inviting the entire clan over without checking with me!

Ramit

I think we'll have to settle for IVF. Mona is so angry, there is no way she'll let me come close anytime soon.

Mona

The Deols of Delhi are descending upon us for dinner tonight. I've spent every waking hour of the last two days cleaning the house and all of today getting the food ready.

There are six cousins in Delhi currently. Three of them have children. One of them, Mohini, is expecting. One, Chiku, is newly married and will probably be expecting before we know it. Suttu is in college and hopefully isn't expecting. Plus there's Nayantara, Daisy chachi's daughter-in-law, and her two brats.

And I have no full-time help! Which means I will be perpetually in the kitchen, microwaving food.

Laila Sachdev gets caterers, waiters, decorators and bartenders for her party. And look at me: all-in-one!

Mummy is very happy. She's called me ten times since yesterday to enquire about the preparations, and has even told me which china to use. Hasn't spoken about baby-making even once. Must be really, *really* excited.

Mom has called to show her sympathy and tsk-tsk at the large family I've married into. She still finds it hard to keep a track of who's-who in the Deol family.

Ramit has set up the bar in the corner and looks even more miserable than I do – if that's possible. He has a presentation on Monday, which he's brooding over. He shouldn't have let Mummy talk him into this dinner.

I'm also a little worried, because the Deols are a very loud lot. If the Sachdevs see them, we're never getting invited to their parties ever again. Not like I want to go. As long as they send over the leftovers. And tell me what wine it was I had almost a bottle of.

Tina Tej Mushran, Laila's friend, called to invite me for some party again. Spoke for over forty-five minutes about things I couldn't follow at all – some celeb party she went to and some caterers who were excellent and that she's hiring for her own party and all that jazz. She also purred about how lovely it was to have Laila move back to Delhi after all these years and how they'd known each other since college, though they didn't go to the same college and only met through their ex-boyfriends. She then enquired about Ramit and my relationship, stuff that I didn't have time to shed light on. Hung up after telling her that though we had other commitments, we'll try to make it to her party.

Anyway, now the bheed is coming over and I've drawn the curtains so that the Sachdevs don't get to see the tamasha that is definitely going to happen. Also don't want the nosy Deols to chance upon the Sachdev's living-room love-making.

Oh God. We should call the Sachdev's over soon to return the favour. And now I'll have to invite Tina Tej Mushran too. Argh! But no way would I combine them with the Deols.

Ramit

Mona shot me a look of horror before running upstairs to change the moment the bell rang.

Can't believe I've let my mother bully me into this.

Mona

So the dinner.

It was as loud and messy as I had feared. There were screaming children; one photo frame was broken; one of the nephews has just started school and was made to recite *Twinkle Twinkle* on loop by his unreasonably proud parents. There was a diaper in my kitchen bin even though there's a bin in the loo. And Mohini was being dramatic and refusing to eat anything since she's pregnant – I had to make her soup. Then she threw it all up in the guest bathroom.

The adults were having a 'rocking' time. Someone had decided to take the party to the garden. Somesh tayi's daughter-in-law kept running her hand over my paunch and asking about 'good news'. I disappointed her rather bluntly and ignored her the rest of the time.

I was stuck in the kitchen all evening and my legs were killing me. They still are. Newly-married Chiku had offered to help out in the kitchen but all she did was gossip about the Daisy chachi fiasco. Then she bitched about Mohini having a honeymoon baby. Actually, she sounded a bit wistful. I don't think she got too much action on her own honeymoon. She also watched me closely for my reaction but I purposely refused to meet her eyes. I think all she did was wipe one serving plate before I heaped the paneer tikka on it. So much for helping out.

Ramit popped in every now and then to ask how he could help. He looked like he was having a nervous breakdown himself. He also looked guilty about having such a large family. He bloody well should.

I told him to get the napkins out with the cheeseballs.

He wanted to know where we keep the napkins.

Then he wanted to know whether he should take out the white or printed ones.

Then he wanted to know which tray he should take the cheeseballs out on.

Then he wanted to know how to take the cheeseballs out of the kadhai.

Then he didn't know where the serving spoons were kept.

I just told him to return to the bar and take care of everyone's drinks. I also requested him to get Chiku out of my hair, which at least he did successfully.

There was a brief moment in the kitchen when Ramit sweetly walked in and hugged me. I wanted to melt in his arms. And then he kissed me.

'Hai! So sweet!' we heard Suttu say. We retracted.

God! The Deols!

They're just everywhere!

Ramit

I hadn't realized how exhausted Mona was till she slept through the weekend. Wonder if she even ate at that dinner.

Laila called to find out if we were going to Tina's party. I had no idea we'd been invited but told her Mona wasn't feeling well.

All this gave me time to work on my presentation though. Of course, at that, Mona's head finally emerged from the covers to call me a workaholic.

Week 5

If you haven't had your period yet, take a test

Mona

Woke up at 9.00 a.m. Ramit was dressed and ready to go to office. I shouted some instructions to Lakshmi about what to make for breakfast and went back to sleep. Don't think Ramit missed me at the breakfast table. He had his damned phone for company.

Ramit

Just realized while driving that our maid's name is Lakshmi. That makes her Lakshmibai. Jhansi ki Rani! Reached office and texted Mona my joke.

No response. Guess she's still sour about bheed night.

Mona

Finally pulled myself out of bed at noon before Lakshmi left.

Ate breakfast, showered, switched on the television and fell asleep again.

Planning to sue the Deols for my condition.

Ramit

Checked my phone twice during the meeting. Still no response.

Meri family divorce karake chhodegi.

Mona

Sat up in bed at 3.00 p.m. finally with my heart in my mouth. Something was wrong. I don't typically remember my date but I was pretty sure I was late.

Debated whether I should get myself a pregnancy test. Or whether I should wait another day.

Lay in bed till 4.00 p.m. Decided to get on with it and walk to a chemist. Decided not to tell Ramit. He'd get over-excited, and it might be a false alarm.

Then spent half an hour deciding which chemist to go to.

The one within our condo knows everyone. I'd be the gossip of the colony.

There was one down the road but it is always overcrowded with these men hanging around the nearby wine and beer shop.

There was one at the mall but the mall's too far, and I was still tired from the bheed dinner.

Then remembered the one in S-block market. It was typically empty at this hour, and no one there would know me.

Finally settled on that and left.

I wonder if men feel the same way when they buy condoms.

Ramit

Still no reply from Mona.

Told Surjit the joke. He laughed so hard coke spurted from his nostrils. That's the kind of recognition I deserve. Still, it was pretty disgusting.

Mona

Drove to the S-Block market chemist and waited in the car. It was surprisingly busy. The next-door grocery store had a huge crowd too. Seriously. Who are these people? Don't they go to work? Sleep? Watch TV in the afternoon? Anything?

I pretended to read something on my phone as I walked to the shop, looking at inconsequential WhatsApp forwards and responding to an odd one here and there to avoid catching anyone's eye. I'm sure I looked horribly guilty.

There were two other people milling around the chemist's counter, discussing cricket. Then the guy behind the counter raised his eyebrows at me in question.

I cleared my throat confidently.

'One Vicks Vaporub, one Saradon, one Crocin and ... one pregnancy test.'

'What?'

Stupid, deaf chemist!

'Pregnancy test,' I hissed.

'Pregnancy test?' he repeated loudly.

I nodded and felt my cheeks burning with embarrassment. I could see a few heads turn to look at me. I quickly put my hand on the counter, drumming my fingers impatiently so that my large wedding ring with all its sixteen diamonds were on display, and cursed myself a little bit for not wearing something else that would certify me as married. Do I even own a mangalsutra?

'Pregnancy test!' the guy hollered to his assistant, much to my horror. The moron! He didn't call out for Saradon and Vicks and Crocin but this one he wants his *champu* to fetch!

My face was burning by the time the packet arrived at the counter and he discreetly shoved it into a brown paper envelope, just like they do with sanitary napkins. Too late for discretion.

I didn't even bother checking the price or brand or the date of expiry and just shoved the whole thing into my bag. I quickly dished out the exact amount and banged it on the counter top and walked out, avoiding all the curious eyes on me, my knees shaking a little.

When I got home, the real terror set in.

Ramit

Like not even a smiley. She's read it. Double blue ticks.

It was a good joke.

Mona

What the hell! All that trouble at the chemist and I've only bought ONE test. ONE. What if this one goes wrong? How stupid are you, Mona Deol?

* * *

I'm not sure why I'm avoiding it, but here I am watching a re-run of *MasterChef Australia* to while away time. Like I'll magically get my period or get pregnant as the seconds tick by.

* * *

Okay. This is it.

Don't get all excited, Mona. You may have just forgotten your dates.

* * *

I know it's just six lines of instructions but I wanted to be sure. I couldn't waste this test. I spent ten minutes reading it. Ok, fifteen. Or twenty. My hands were trembling.

So, I guess I need to find a container to pee in. One can't pee on a stick, directly! You're to pee and put two drops of the pee on the … ugh! So gross!

* * *

Oh bloody hell! I spent twenty minutes reading the damned instructions and still missed reading how the first pee of the morning is the best to measure HCG, which is the presence of pregnancy hormones.

But now it's already done, and it was disgusting! So awkward, and I didn't really know how to … position myself. Oh God! I just want to wash my hands and never go through this again.

What is my life coming to?

Ramit

Radio silence from Mona. She can't be holding a grudge against me about the party, can she?

Mona

Finally mustered up the courage to look at the test. Those were definitely two lines. Two. Lines.

Oh God …

Ramit

7.00 p.m. Nothing from Mona.

This is trouble.

Mona

I don't even remember what I'd mumbled to Lakshmi about dinner. I hope it's not bhindi. It's probably bhindi. I think she does it purposely, making strange smelly bhindi to piss me off. I'll have to do something about it. I don't remember hating bhindi so much in our previous house.

Why am I thinking about bhindi?

Ramit

Left office early. Mona was sitting on the bed holding a piece of paper.

She shoved it at me. It didn't look like a suicide note, so that was a relief. It was more like an instruction sheet for … oh!

I couldn't believe it. Then she handed me the stick.

'I read it right, right?' she asked softly.

I looked at the instructions and studied the stick.

'Ramit?'

'Mona ...'

'Is it?'

'I think so ... yes.'

We both sat there wordlessly for a while. I wasn't sure what I was supposed to feel.

'We should meet the doctor tomorrow,' Mona broke the silence.

I agreed. Asked if we should tell Mummy, and then immediately regretted it. Thankfully, she didn't register that bit.

Mona

The fact that Ramit was holding a stick which had my urine on was a little nauseating. Or maybe the nausea is all in my head now that I realize I'm ... PREGNANT!

OH MY GOD!

Ramit

We debated about which gynaec to go to. I, against my good sense yet again, suggested we ask Roshini, my cousin's wife, but Mona snapped my head off, saying what if it's a false alarm and Roshini gets all blurty and calls back to find out how it went.

So she called up some friend and got the number of one Dr Mehak Khan in Vasant Vihar. I think it's better to meet one closer to Gurgaon but I will not argue with Mona. She looks scary.

Hope she can't tell I'm nervous. Very nervous.

Mona

Ramit is some sort of cool cat. I was wide awake all night but he slept right off! Maybe he thinks this is a false alarm.

We reach the clinic – it has a massive line! – and it hits me that we know absolutely nothing about the doctor.

I say as much to Ramit and he immediately Googles her.

'Look. Decent stuff about her on the net. She's pretty well known. There's even an article where she's been listed among the top ten gynaecologists in Delhi. And didn't your friend Avantika go to her as well?'

I don't reply because Uma Bhasin has just walked in, wearing designer sunglasses and carrying a designer bag and wearing the brightest red lipstick ever. Just like Laila Sachdev. Red lipstick is clearly in.

I immediately turn to study Ramit's phone. I really don't want Uma to notice me.

Uma and I went to school together. I haven't seen her in years. But I don't want to meet anyone I know at a gynaec clinic!

'Mona Mathur!'

My heart sinks to my toes.

'Uma?' I hear myself squeak.

'Hi!' She gives me a hug and an air kiss. How very *Delhi* of her! 'How've you been?'

'I'm good!'

'So, are you pregnant?'

Oh God! Bloody direct as always. She eyes my belly – just like Somesh tayiji and her intrusive children! And ever since that positive test last night, I anyhow feel like I've put on about 100kgs just on my stomach!

I adjust my top a little and give a little laugh.

'No, no. Just a routine check. What about you?'

'Oh, I already have a three-year-old. No more! No more!' She laughs.

Right! What are we supposed to say next? Ramit is so engrossed in his phone that he hasn't even noticed Uma, I think.

'Is that your husband?' she asks.

'Yes. Ramit.' He finally looks up. 'Ramit, this is my friend Uma. Uma and I went to school together.'

'Hi,' Ramit smiles at us, his fingers still lingering on his phone.

'Mona and I were so close in school. Such good friends,' she informs Ramit. Liar! We were hardly friends!

'Do you guys stay here in Vasant Vihar?' she asks chirpily.

'No, we stay in Gurgaon,' I said.

'Oh. We stay in VV. My husband's into construction.' People who move to Delhi really do become Delhi. Who asked her what her husband is *into*? 'What are you doing now?' she continues.

'I work with a travel company,' for some reason, I lie. 'What about you?'

'Oh I'm into bags. I export for Dior, Gucci ...'

She goes on and on about her work, but all I can think about is who she hung out with in school and who she could possibly be in touch with and who would eventually know about my visit to the gynaec and then discuss my conception issues …

And just then, thankfully, we are called in.

When we go inside, I am expecting a team of doctors in green overalls and face masks hovering around. Or at least a lady in a lab coat. And maybe a few charts of the uterus. Or at least an experienced, grey-haired doctor who looks like a grandmother and will regale us with tales of her grandchildren.

Instead we come face to face with a sparkling woman in a white shirt and fitting jeans, wearing these cool blue glasses and – she's so chic, and doesn't look a day older than us. She might actually be younger! She shakes my hand as if this is a business meeting.

'Hi. Mona? I'm Dr Mehak. Take a seat.'

Ramit

Oh. The doctor, she's quite … good-looking.

Can feel Mona eyeing me, and realize I'm staring. Shake my head. Must focus on the important stuff.

Still, hadn't expected this.

Mona

That was a pretty intense check-up. I got quizzed on a lot of things. Medical history, diet, lifestyle etc. Ramit did not speak a word. I could've simply gone alone. He wasn't buried in his phone, thankfully. He just looked stiff. Sat with his back straight, like we were in the principal's office. He looked a bit embarrassed for having knocked me up, I think.

I told the doctor about the pregnancy test and how I hadn't done it first thing in the morning as the instructions said I should. She kept nodding without looking up at me.

'Okay then. I'm just going to put down a blood test for you.' She noted something in her notepad, in very doctor-like handwriting. 'You get this done today and repeat it after two days.'

'Right … right…' I mumbled.

'Umm …' I heard Ramit finally open his mouth. 'So, is she pregnant?'

Dr Mehak smiled at him. 'The right term is, are *we* pregnant. Well, the pregnancy test says so, you say. But it's best to confirm through a blood test. Especially since you're only a week late, isn't it? But you aren't completely sure of your date?'

I felt extremely stupid.

'This blood test will tell us, then.' She smiled.

So, basically, another three days before we'll really know.

Ramit

Never Google medical stuff.

We got the first report in and didn't know what the ranges meant and I Googled it. It means Mona is either pregnant or terminally ill.

She's looking rather pale, staring into her phone's blue screen now. I think she's been Googling too.

Week 6

By now, the first symptom of pregnancy – nausea or breast tenderness – makes its appearance. You may also feel tired and urinate more frequently

Mona

I'm pregnant. Without a single symptom. No filmy chakkar, no filmy fainting, no puking, no sign of nausea whatsoever. But Dr Mehak has just told us that I'm pregnant. That *we* are pregnant.

I have been peeing a lot, though. I suppose that's a symptom. I didn't bother asking Dr Mehak.

Anyway, should I be calling anything a *symptom*? Pregnancy isn't a disease, after all.

Ramit kept saying 'I can't believe it' all the way home, and I kept oscillating between feeling totally excited and totally nervous. He even offered to take the day off, but changed his mind before I could jump at it.

Anyway, it looks like this is it. In another nine months, we'll have a baby.

I called my mother when I got home. And didn't get the reaction I was expecting. She first went really silent and then spoke in hushed tones.

'Don't tell anyone till you complete three months, okay?'

'Why?' I whispered back.

'Anything can happen!' Mom said ominously.

Trust my mother to get all negative about the one *good* news she's been waiting for.

'But I have to tell Ramit's mother!'

Mom hesitated. 'Okay, you can tell her,' she said finally. 'But don't go blabbering it all out to everyone else. These Deols ...' She tutted. 'Now, listen to me. You don't do anything to stress yourself. No physical exercise. No lifting heavy stuff. You haven't lifted anything heavy, have you?'

Oh God! I realized I've spent all of last month shifting and carrying cartons of stuff here and there. If only that Shania had lifted a finger...

'No alcohol,' she instructed.

I wanted to tell her if it hadn't been for all that wine at Laila Sachdev's party, there would've been no baby at all.

'Always sit with your feet up. Take complete bed rest.'

'But ... why?'

'Because you have to be extra careful in the first three months.'

'Mom, the doctor said I should live like any normal person.'

'Don't listen to the doctor. Listen to your mother. I've had two children. And your pregnancy is precious. Now don't go up and down the stairs all the time. Get a full-time maid. Should I send Rani to you?'

'No. I already have a maid.'

'She's part-time.'

'Relax!'

'Are you feeling sick?'

'No.'

'Why aren't you feeling sick?'

'I don't know!'

'You're supposed to feel sick. Have lime.'

'But I'm not sick!'

'And no heels.'

My mother is ridiculous. I hung up on her and called Ramit's Mummy.

She was no better. Insisted that we be discreet, and keep it a secret.

'Have adrak.' she said.

'Why?'

'To help with the sickness.'

'But I'm not feeling sick.'

'You will.'

This is the response I get for giving them the news they've been waiting for these last four years? Have adrak? Don't wear heels? Don't tell anyone?

I called Shania. Disconnected. Dialled again. Disconnected.

Something seemed to be wrong. The caller tune had changed to some *Om Shaanti Shaanti* bhajan.

Anyway, had to pee, so stopped trying.

Ramit

'Ramit, you have to be careful!'

That's what my mother called to tell me – no congratulations, or rather, no thank you, for giving them the one thing they've been waiting for all these years.

She's even refused to tell Papa, lest he tell Bade Papa.

Bade Papa, Somesh tayiji's husband, is the patriarch of the family. We rarely keep secrets from him.

But Mummy has insisted on making this some FBI agenda.

Mona

Shania called back. She claims she knew I was going to tell her I'm pregnant because she's into meditation and shit now and she can feel the energies talking to her.

Trust my sister to go cuckoo at the one time I need her to tell my mom to back off.

Ramit

Apparently Mona has switched off her phone. The mothers have hounded me with calls and messages since.

Mummy: No more Colas for Mona. She should stay off aerated drinks.

Mom: Chinese food is a big no-no. It has Ajinomoto. Bad for baby's brain development.

Mummy: Get her ginger toffees. It's a must.

Mom: Give her a glass of milk thrice a day. It's a must.

Mummy: No foot massage. It has some pressure points that could induce early labour.

Mom: Put up a picture of a cute baby in the room.

Mummy: Put up your bachpan ka photo in the room.

Mom: Is she throwing up?

Mummy: Is she throwing up?

Turned the phone off. Mailed clients to call me on my landline.

Mona

For some reason, Ramit thought I'd gone off to buy him an anniversary present today, and was planning a surprise or something. I had almost forgotten tomorrow's our anniversary in the first place! I've spent the day peeing and sleeping.

And how dare he want an anniversary present? I'm giving him a baby!

Ramit

Mummy called at seven in the morning on our anniversary.

'I know you have tickets for *Dhai-Dhishoom* booked for tonight. You can't go for it.'

No happy anniversary. Five years of marriage and a grandchild on its way, but I don't even get a happy anniversary. Just an order that I can't go for a movie. As if I'm in school and need her permission.

'Why not?' I asked defiantly, sounding braver than I felt.

'Too much violence. I want Mona to think only happy thoughts,' she said sternly. 'And anyway, don't ask me why not! I'm your mother.'

'But she likes watching movies and this one has that actor she loves, and she's really looking forward to it ...'

'Ramit!'

No one messes with Mummy.

I told Mona we couldn't go.

Turns out, no one messes with a pregnant Mona either.

Off to the movies we went.

Mona

We ran into Tina Tej Mushran at the theatre. She looked like she was going clubbing instead of the movies. She had on a glittery tank top and a denim jacket. I instinctively put my hand on my stomach, lest she notice I'm pregnant and tell people. Even Ramit's ears turned pink with the stress. Or maybe at the sight of her cleavage. Ramit should've been born in the fourteenth century.

We made small talk and she invited me to drinks next week at her place. Said something about calling some caterers and the way she talked, it seemed like the caterers came first and the guests, second. She said that Laila Sachdev would be coming too. I made some weak excuse. I can't be drinking. But now they'll think I'm too uncool to hang out with them and I'll be stuck with the likes of Mrs Kapoor, who haw-haws the likes of Laila Sachdev (which even I do but I'm more subtle about it).

Now I'm sulking. And eating some caramel popcorn in the hall which, by the way, tastes like lead.

Caught Ramit looking at me strangely. Think he finds it a little unappealing to watch me gobble through a tub of gross popcorn.

But now that I'm … sorry … now that *we* are pregnant, he can find me as unappealing as he wants!

Ramit

Mummy called during the movie and I had to disconnect. If she overheard the background score she would have killed me for bringing Mona to the movie, after all. Then she called on Mona's phone.

Told Mona to speak to her on one of her loo visits.

Why is she perpetually in the loo?

Mona

I hope this whole urinating thing is a part of pregnancy. Or I have serious bladder issues. I suppose I should ask Dr Mehak.

God! Why does Ramit have to drink that Coke so loudly? He's slurping away so loudly I can barely hear anything.

And I want that Coke. So badly. Considering snatching it out of Ramit's hands.

In an attempt to distract myself, I keep sipping water every time he has a sip of his Coke. Just to numb my senses.

Ramit

No wonder Mona was running to the loo all the time. She was guzzling down a full bottle of water every five minutes.

And now she wants me to drive really fast and get home because she wants to pee.

Mona

I can't believe we didn't pay attention to our bathroom before. Why don't I have better tiles? Why haven't I bothered getting better toiletries? Why are the towels so unpretty?

Now that I seem to be spending a significant part of my life peeing, I'm beginning to see how it needs some serious revamping.

Ramit

Google says Mona's kidneys are working overtime to keep the system clean and there's a growing uterus putting pressure on her bladder. At least it's not kidney failure.

Google also says she should have lots of water.

Went into the garage and brought out one of those old-school Mayur jugs we'd been given in Amritsar. But she wants to drink from our purple Tupperware bottle only.

Mona can really be like her mother sometimes. Pseudo-snob.

Mona

A Mayur jug! Must've been his mother's suggestion. Who uses that any more? Security guards?

All I'm doing is drinking and peeing. Yesterday, I had eighteen glasses of water.

Also used up two toilet paper rolls and one full handwash last week.

And the puking hasn't even started!

Week 7

You are in the throes of nausea

Mona

'I threw a what?'

'Are you in the throes of nausea?' Ramit's Mummy asked. Seriously, having an English teacher–cum–ex-principal is not fun.

'I don't have any nausea.'

'You're not feeling sick?'

That's what nausea means, Mummy! I wanted to yell. But I just said, 'no,' politely.

Then my mom called.

'You're still not feeling sick?'

'No.'

'Why?'

'How am I supposed to know?'

She sounded very suspicious.

Then Ramit asked.

'You're sure you're not feeling sick?'

'I'll tell you what I'm sick of ... it's that question. I'm not sick! What should I do? Shove two fingers down my throat?'

Ramit

Mummy is very upset that Mona is not throwing up. She suggested that I speak to the doctor about it. I spent the morning calming her down.

If that carton of caramel popcorn didn't make her throw up last week, nothing will.

Mona keeps snapping at me for asking her how she's feeling.

Mona

'So you still haven't started throwing up? That's good. Just eight months of puking for you then.'

'Shania! Why will I be puking for nine months?'

'Arrey! They show na in Hindi movies.'

Hindi movies have forever ruined the meaning of pregnancy. They show women puking the minute they conceive, and then massive bellies the very next day. And of course, the *chakkar.* You're expected to suddenly hold your head and faint dramatically in your husband's arms and call a doctor home who can check your *pulse* and declare you pregnant. I had to get a blood test. I feel cheated.

'So, di, send me your photo, na. Are you showing?'

I was showing even before I was pregnant, according to Somesh tayiji and her nosey daughter-in-law.

'When are you coming back from the ashram? What are you doing there in the first place?' I attempted to change the subject.

'I met this guy …'

It had to be a man! This boy-crazy sister of mine!

Ramit

'But why isn't she feeling sick?' Mummy hissed at me.

I threw some research at her. Told her that 30% women get no nausea or morning sickness during their pregnancy.

She became indignant. Went on about knowing more than me. Insisted I ask the doctor.

Mona

Is he bloody serious? I'm not going to the doctor to ask her why I'm *not* barfing!

Anyway, woke up feeling a little grubby. I think it's the spices Lakshmi put in the bloody bhindi. Cannot stand bhindi. Why is there bhindi in the house in the first place? Because of our beloved Lakshmibai. It's her weapon, Ramit claims. He really needs to get over this stupid joke.

Told Ramit I wasn't feeling good and didn't bother going down for breakfast.

But later when I went downstairs, found Ramit gleefully whispering on the phone with his Mum.

'She was feeling a little sick.' I saw him smile. 'Yes. Yes. I know.'

Blasted him for being happy about me feeling sick. Told him to get me lime and ginger and a bag I could puke into. Felt perfectly fine within half an hour. Everyone's disappointed in me again.

***

Caught Ramit whispering on the phone again with Mummy.

'Yes. She's started showing a little.'

Stormed into the room and made him put down the phone.

He murmured something about mood swings. I wanted to hurl my shoe at him.

Ramit

My wife is now officially crazy.

Week 8

Around this time, your blood circulation steadily increases

Ramit

So Mona's obviously doing fine, other than wanting to bite my head off. I'm getting high blood pressure with all her screaming.

So, decided to get out and play a round of tennis with Shashi Sachdev.

They're quite warm, the Sachdevs. When we didn't go for Tina's party, Laila sent Mona a bunch of flowers the next day. And they keep stopping by the garden to say hello.

And obviously, I can see that Mona has a massive crush on Shashi.

I should build some muscle.

Mona

Milind-Shashi came to the house today. Don't know if my head swooned at the sight of him in his shorts or if it was my pregnancy acting up.

I sat in the living room for a long time, imagining him playing tennis. And later, blocking out images of him unbuttoning Laila Sachdev's shirt.

Ramit

Got such a fright when I got back. Lying on our living room carpet was Mona, an open book in her hand. I shook her several times and even felt her pulse. She thankfully stirred and told me to stop being crazy – she was just a little sleepy post lunch.

Pressed her and she admitted to feeling woozy, and needing to lie down. She says it's nothing, but I don't care – I'm taking her to the doctor.

Mona

The doctor says that apparently, some pregnant women do feel faint.

I finally feel like a Bollywood heroine and have something to report back to the paranoid mothers.

Of course, as soon as they heard this, both promptly started freaking out.

Mummy declared she would take the Monday morning Shatabdi.

Mom decided to send Rani, our help in Dehradun, by the Monday evening Shatabdi. Good, because I prefer Rani to either of the mothers any day. But then Ramit told her that there was no need and that his mother was coming on Monday morning.

My bechari type mum got competitive – if Ramit's mother can come to serve her daughter-in-law, she can do the same for her flesh and blood. Now both mothers will be here on Monday.

I wanted to faint at the thought of it. Told Ramit to sort it out.

Ramit

Convinced both parties to come one after the other, so that Mona would have someone with her at all times.

A calendar of sorts has been drawn up. Mummy arrives next Monday for two weeks on the pretext of helping us set up the house – that's what the Deols of Amritsar are being told.

Mona's Mom arrives for two weeks post that, followed by two weeks of Shania.

By then the first trimester will be over.

Then Rani can move in.

Mona

Got an earful from Mom – about how she's my mother and Ramit's 'Mummy' is my mother-in-*law*. How could I be so unfair as to have her over with me first instead of my own mother!

Didn't have the stamina to argue. Hung up.

Ramit

Got an earful from Mummy about how it's unfair that our part of the family only gets two weeks and Mona's family gets four.

Didn't have the patience to argue. Hung up.

Mona

Lakshmi barged into my bedroom without knocking just as I was taking my bra off. No regard for privacy whatsoever. Excitedly told me I had a guest.

So here I am, bra back on, sitting across Tina Tej Mushran, pulling my T-shirt a bit lower on my tummy so that she doesn't notice anything. She pulls out, much to my horror, her Virginia Slims-type cigarette holder and a cigarette.

I rack my brains on how to stop her when I spot the portly Lakshmi sputtering around the kitchen.

'Actually, I'm so sorry,' I say hurriedly, 'but my cook, she's pregnant and I don't allow smoking in the house for her well-being.'

Tina raises one perfectly shaped eyebrow in surprise and I quickly give her this angelic smile.

'That's rather kind of you, Mona.' She thankfully stuffs the cigarette back into the case. 'Gosh! I was off smokes during my pregnancies,' she tells me, holding her forehead dramatically. 'It's so bloody tough. The toughest part of the pregnancy.' She clearly didn't have the fainting spells. Or any of the puking the mothers are waiting with bated breath for.

'Anyway, thought I'd come sit with you till Laila comes home from work. She'll be here in another half an hour, so we have time for a little chit-chat? Down to the point, why have you been avoiding me, love?'

'Sorry?' I splutter.

'I invited you and your husband to two of my parties and you didn't show up. What seems to be the issue?'

I adjust my T-shirt again and prop a cushion in front of me. 'Oh, nothing at all. I've just had this terrible stomach bug so I was so off eating out and alcohol and you know how it is.'

Right. That was weak!

But she nods understandingly. 'Oh yes. Tummy bugs are the worst. My husband Tej had jaundice way back in 2009 and he had to stay off alcohol for months. I told him very clearly, you can stop coming to the club if you like, darling, but asking me to give up alcohol for you is really a test of love.' She laughs and curls her legs up on my brand new sofas *without* taking off her shoes. I feel faint at the sight of it but try to look nonchalant.

'So, how long before your bug goes away?' she asks.

'It could take a while.'

'Oh too bad. I believe Laila was planning to have another one of her parties next month to celebrate Shashi's birthday, but guess you'll be laid up in bed. Did I tell you about the party they had for her birthday?'

She rattles on, and I keep nodding as Lakshmibai lays out this impressive tray of goodies I had no idea she knew how to cook! There are pakodas and halwa and these shiny chicken chunks in schezwan sauce and tall glasses of mint iced tea. And here I am being fed bhindi for every freaking meal!

She is clearly out to impress Tina, who is sitting there with her stilettoes digging into my sofa. I tap my feet so that she can notice how *my* feet are on the floor, but she stays completely oblivious.

'Laila's also been a bit sick, you know,' Tina says. 'I think it's all the travel. I think she ate something on the flight. I never eat on these domestic flights, even when I'm travelling business. I eat at the lounge. We're platinum card holders.'

It is a miracle I manage to stay awake through this conversation.

Ramit

Got home to find a very tired Mona. And an assortment of snacks. I asked her where it came from and she said Lakshmibai had cooked it all for Tina Tej Mushran.

She also told me that Dr Mehak has suggested we get a dating scan. Mona's scheduled it for morning, before Mummy arrives. Better that way, because there is no way Mummy won't come along if she's here.

Week 9

A dating scan is a more precise way of establishing your due date

Mona

For my sister Shania, a dating scan would probably mean scanning a room to see who is date-worthy material. To me it is clearly an ultrasound to date the pregnancy. I'm ready. I've Googled it all. I've had plenty of water so that my bladder is full and they can look into my insides.

We are made to fill out some forms and Ramit looks over my shoulder.

'What's LMP?' he asks.

'Last Menstrual Period,' I revel in my newly acquired knowledge.

Ramit turns beetroot red.

I roll my eyes at him. Are all men embarrassed about the word 'menstrual' or is it just Ramit? How silly!

'That's what they typically ask in a scan, by the way,' I pass on some more of my knowledge. 'They always want to know about the LMP.'

Ramit nods, trying to be all mature about it, but I can see him twitching to take out his phone and bury himself in it.

'But …' I add, 'When someone asks you, please just say how many weeks pregnant we are, not the LMP. That's only for the doctor.'

He looks at me strangely, like I'm doubting his intelligence.

'Do you calculate from when the period starts or ends?' he asks, so softly I have to read his lips to understand.

Shit. Forgot to check that. Now I'm confused too.

Ramit

We're fourth in line despite an appointment.

Then we're hustled into this dark room and Mona is covered with a white sheet and the lights are all turned off. But there's no sign of the doctor. It seems like a good time to reply to an email but Mona snaps at me when I take out my phone.

Mona

I had to lie on the table for about ten minutes. The nurse slid the waistband of my trousers down but I pulled them right back up once she left to bring in the doctor.

Then this large woman in a doctor's coat and dark henna-dyed hair came in, looking rather bored. I squirmed. Ramit had sneaked out his phone. I caught his eye and glared at him.

'LMP?' the doctor yawned.

'I think twelfth December,' I said timidly.

She raised her pencilled eyebrow at me. She reminded me of Shahnaz Husain.

'You think?'

'I'm not sure …' I mumbled guiltily.

She turned back to her screen and typed in something slowly.

Then she put some gel on her device and moved it around my abdomen. I couldn't make out a thing on the screen in front of me, let alone a baby! I raised my head higher to see if I was missing something, but it was all just fuzzy static in black and white.

My heart skipped a beat. Was I even pregnant?

Ramit

All I could see were white lines and black blobs, like TV static.

The doctor announced that she would have to do an internal, and shoved a towel into my hand.

She told Mona to empty her bladder.

Mona

Till now, there was a certain privacy I'd enjoyed in life. And sure, I know there are some things that come with pregnancy. But being asked to take off my pants … and panties (!!!) … off! Well, not something I thought I'd have to do, not before the delivery, anyway.

I stood there, trembling as the nurse held this sheet as a curtain between me and Shahnaz Husain. I tried to remember the last time I'd waxed my legs.

Then she shoved the damned thing up … me.

'Relax,' Shahnaz Husain told me, as she gazed at the screen. I wanted to punch her. Seriously. Relax? Who was she, my mother-in-law?

'This is better,' she announced finally. I still didn't know what she was talking about. 'You can call her husband in,' she told the nurse.

Ramit walked in like a zombie and immediately turned red, seeing me in that state.

There were all sorts of amoeba-like shapes on the computer screen now.

'That's the baby, can you see?' Shahnaz Husain sounded slightly bored.

I frowned at the screen. I wasn't sure what the hell I was supposed to see. But then the doctor zoomed in, and there was something of an outline – it looked like a big black patch.

I turned to Ramit.

Ramit

I didn't know what was going on.

Mona

Poor, poor Ramit. He kept frowning at the screen and pushing up his glasses. He even took off his glasses, cleaned them and went closer to the screen.

'But … it's a blob,' he finally said to the doctor.

'Well, not really,' said Shahnaz Husain, offended at the observation. 'It's more like a tadpole at this point of time.'

I tried not to think about it. I'd rather think of a blob inside me than a tadpole.

'If you look closely, here, you can see the heart beat.'

She zoomed in, and some blue and red dots appeared on the screen. I could see a faint beat, all right. I would've been totally excited by that, had Ramit not looked so lost squinting at the screen.

I held his hand and pointed to the screen from my awkward lying down position.

'There ... can you see it? That change of colour?'

He just frowned at the screen, his eyes moving from one corner to the other. He obviously couldn't figure out a thing.

'This is the first picture of your baby,' Shahnaz Husain drawled her practiced script. 'Isn't it exciting?' She made it sound like anything but.

I quickly changed my expression since Ramit's gave away nothing but confusion. I didn't want to be the type of mother who couldn't see the miracle of her child.

'I'll make you hear the heartbeat next time. That's all for now.'

Ramit and I looked at each other unsurely.

I don't think he's coming for any more ultrasounds.

Ramit

My school principal mother has never shouted at me. Before.

The minute I pick her up from the station, she furiously throws her bag in and barges into the passenger seat, tugging at her seat belt with all her might. I know I'm an hour late, but we were at the ultra sound and ... Oh.

Mona

Mummy is soooooo angry at us for not telling her about the dating scan. Unlike my mother, who almost wept out of self-pity that we only told her about the scan after we'd seen the results, Mummy had no time for tears – only pointless screaming. Ramit came in looking like a giant tomato, simply placed her bags in the guest room and stood sheepishly in a corner. I was afraid about what was in store for me, but instead I got a giant hug and a kiss on the forehead.

'Is he taking good care of you? Is he? Is he?' she asked threateningly, holding me by my shoulders. I quickly nodded.

'Ramit, I want you home by 7 p.m. sharp,' she barked at him.

I could see Ramit beginning to say something to her, but then he thought better of it, nodded obediently and dashed out of the house.

'He didn't bother telling me about your scan,' she said gently, taking me by the arm and leading me to the dining area. 'I would have changed my ticket to come yesterday.'

I felt my own ears turning pink. We had both decided against letting the hyperventilating mothers know, but here I was, throwing poor Ramit under the bus.

'Anyway,' she said, taking a seat. 'I believe there's another scan in two weeks? I will go only after that. You can tell your mother she can postpone her tickets.'

Ramit

Mummy was being difficult. She was looking at the ultrasound image, and when I asked if she could see the baby, she snapped a yes. She would never admit to being unable to spot her 'tadpole' grandchild.

She told me the EDD said 7 September.

I didn't ask what EDD stands for. Will Google later.

She complained loudly of there being no nutritious food in the house and admonished me for it. She then grumbled about the need for sunlight and yanked the curtains open to see a scantily clad Laila Sachdev doing yoga – the downward dog pose.

Obviously, Mummy drew the curtains back immediately and stomped off.

Mona

Mummy has taken the house by storm.

I'm being given something to eat every half an hour. When I refuse to eat, saying I'm too full, I'm met with a giant grin instead of the expected frown. She thinks I'm on the brink of puking, and that clearly makes her happy.

She's also majorly transformed our bedroom and brought new furniture for it.

Ramit

Mona has been planted on the bed, with several fluffed-up pillows and strict instructions that she is to go nowhere but the bathroom and back.

Saw a stack of 'What to Expect' books about pregnancy on the table next to the bed, along with a few on handling a toddler. Mummy says it'll give us perspective.

We have two new pictures hanging from the wall. One of baby Krishna eating from a bucket of butter and one of some unknown baby. I'd have assumed Mummy would like a Deol baby's photo up there, but as far as I know, none of the bheed has produced a blonde, blue-eyed baby.

On Mona's bedside table is a framed picture of me, wearing nothing but the sacred black thread on my feet, my family jewels on display as I chew on a toy.

Mummy told me proudly that it's one of my nicest pictures. I firmly tell her to tear it up immediately and stop scarring my pregnant wife.

Once Mummy huffs out of the room, Mona falls against her stack of pillows and wails, 'Your mother insists on coming with us to meet Dr Mehak tomorrow. Get us out of it please!'

Mona

I'm going to hit Ramit. Just as I've calmed down – Mummy agreed to stay home instead of coming along to the doctor's – he's had another thought, and wants me to ask Dr Mehak about it.

Ramit

Mona snapped at me. But it's important to know!

Mona

Clearly, the most embarrassing part of the pregnancy wasn't buying that damned pregnancy kit under those judgemental eyes or lying down on the ultrasound table with my pants down. It was today. It was asking the doctor if we can have sex!

I told Ramit we didn't need to ask, since I'd already Googled it and almost all the websites say that it's okay, but he refuses to believe Google. For everything else in the world he believes it!

So, just like I'd gone to the chemist with a list of medicines when actually all I needed was a pregnancy test, I thought I'd just sneak this question in with a few other milder ones.

'How're you feeling?' Dr Mehak asked me.

'Ummm … I still have those fainting spells I'd told you about.'

'Yes. It happens with a few people. Are you working?'

'No.'

'So that's good. Just lie down for a while whenever you feel faint.'

'That's what I do.'

'Any nausea?'

'No.'

'Okay.'

I rattled off some other ailments like gas, bloating and other non-glamorous stuff.

'Anything else?' she asked me with a polite smile.

I turned to look at Ramit, who wore this innocent expression, pretending we hadn't discussed anything at all. He wasn't even looking at me or at her – just staring into space, blinking, his hands nervously twirling his phone around. I debated dropping the question. Then he caught my eye and raised his eyebrow ever so slightly. That man!

'So … can I … can we … ummm …' Thank God they didn't have me plugged into some sort of ECG machine.

I really should have practiced this a little more in my head. What was an appropriate term to use? Sex? Make out? Make love? Make merry?

'Is it okay … as in safe … you know …to have uh … intercourse?'

Intercourse! Of all the terms to have popped into my head! Why couldn't I have just said sex?

'Sure it's safe!' Dr Mehak said cheerfully.

I finally met her eye and she smiled at me. But I knew what she was thinking. *This horny, knocked-up couple.*

I glanced at Ramit. His ears had turned red again. As if I'd asked the unexpected and embarrassed him. I wanted to whack him!

Week 10

You may have gone up a cup size or
more by now

Mona

There are a lot of things Hindi movies don't show about a pregnancy though. For example, boob pain. It's horrid! And all these aches and pains in your pelvic area.

Told Ramit how my abdomen was hurting. He, as always, went on Google, and then told me it hurt cause my body's expanding to make space for the uterus.

Then he said, 'Wow. The human body is amazing!'

I wanted to share my amazing pain by kicking him.

Ramit

Lakshmibai has been demoted to chef's assistant in the kitchen. Mummy insists on doing all the cooking, since Mona needs her tasty and nutritional food. That mean Mummy is adding pure desi ghee to everything – much to Mona's dismay. Told her to stop complaining about her weight as she can't control it.

I'm not sure what a husband is supposed to say to his wife in this situation. Also … looks like all that weight is going to her boobs.

Mona

I cannot believe it! I'm popping out of my bra. I feel like Pamela Anderson. Except that mine are real. The ugliest bras fit like skanky bikini tops now! And while skinny people can be happy about getting some cleavage, I'm supremely embarrassed about going from size 34 to 36. And apparently this is not the end. Am I going to be one of those ladies who go to the lingerie shop and ask for size 44DD?

Ramit

I've told her I can barely notice the expansion but Mona insists Mummy's been looking at her in embarrassment.

Mona

This afternoon, Mummy returned from the market with some thirty scarves for me. She made me stand in front of the mirror and draped them around me in a way that my massive boobs were hidden. I was so right. She *had* noticed them. So damn embarrassing!

Thank God she's stepping out tonight to meet and spend the night at Ruha maasi's.

Ramit

Not just the boobs, anyway. It's also her ...

Mona

Not only is Ramit married to Pamela Anderson, apparently he's also married to Kim Kardashian. Have you seen the size of my butt?

I've got the perfect figure – but for someone tall and dreamy. It's hardly the look for someone who's short and round all over.

My body's new shape is obviously haunting me, so much so that I'm having nightmares about it. I dreamt we were at some five-star hotel and my breasts got stuck in the revolving doors.

Ramit

Mummy has been encouraged to stay over at maasi's for the weekend so that Mona and I get 'alone' time. I'm off to spend the weekend in office and Mona is sulking as usual.

Mona

Unbelievable!

I was in my tracks, wearing one of the many colourful scarves Mummy got me and wandering around the garden this evening when Laila Sachdev pulled up in her car and walked right into my house with a giant, sympathetic hug.

'How're you doing?' she asked, studying my face. 'Shashi was saying you've been rather unwell and Ramit's mother is here to look after you. In fact, I had wanted to come over earlier, but I had some business travel and then Shashi joined me in Italy ...'

Bloody show off!

I made some polite noises and shrugged her off but then felt guilty and asked her in for tea. Regretted it immediately. I should have said 'drinks' and sounded cooler.

Lakshmi pottered in with two cups of tea and her magical tray of goodies, as a rather happy-looking Laila Sachdev rested her stylish butt on my plastic Neelkamal chair outside. Thank God Mummy wasn't here else she would have not approved of Laila's floral mid-thigh skirt. How can she dress like that to work?

'So what really happened to you?' Laila Sachdev asked me as we sipped tea.

I couldn't say something stupid like food poisoning. You can't call your mother-in-law from another state to help you with food poisoning. So I settled on suspected dengue.

Laila looked confused. 'Dengue? In February? How?'

Oh shit.

'Well, suspected. Not confirmed. Therefore it wasn't. Then they suspected typhoid.'

'Suspected? Are they not sure yet?'

Bloody wannabe doctor!

'Mild typhoid,' I said into my cup.

'Hmmm. I hope you feel better soon,' she said, finally. 'In fact, I haven't been so well myself.'

She was beaming at me.

Ramit

Text from Mona. Laila Sachdev is pregnant. Mona is livid that Laila can happily share her 'good news' while we still have to guard ours.

Mona

I wish I could tell Laila I am pregnant too. Maybe she will know what to do about boob pain.

So jealous of the woman. She gets to gloat about it and I don't. And she found out about it just this morning! I've kept mum for weeks!

I've also become shameless now. I'm sitting with my bra open – of course underneath my T-shirt – with my mother-in-law around the house. There is nothing sexy about having large boobs. I've put away all my strapless, backless, underwired bras. Only cotton ones can survive this weight.

When can I start asking real people for advice instead of Google?

And to think of it, it's actually in the first trimester that you really need advice, and that's just when this whole thing is supposed to be all hush-hush.

What a pain this Laila is.

Week 11

Estrogen can make your sense of smell much stronger

Ramit

Mona has turned into some sort of bloodhound. She can smell things from miles away.

I've been made to not only brush but also floss *and* use mouthwash before getting into bed, because Mummy served me a raw onion salad tonight and I had it. Sue me.

And now Mona's punishing me by covering her nose like I'm toxic.

Well, she's the one who keeps farting away and then giggling before informing me that it's the baby, not her.

Very convenient to blame the tadpole for turning her into a hot air balloon. And I'm not allowed to let out even a tiny, innocent, odourless bubble of a fart.

Mona

I think it's a tad dramatic of Ramit to take the pillow with him. He knows very well Mummy's room has an extra pillow. Not like I really told him to leave the room. I just told him to let his digestive system work inside him for a change.

I could smell the onions and the chicken curry. Speaking of which, I am so disappointed. I think this child is vegetarian. I'm just so done with chicken.

Both the mothers think I should have lots of chicken because it's protein and good for me, and Mummy even said it's okay to have it on a Tuesday.

It is a great *dhakka* to the family. Has our carnivore actually given up chicken? Is she going insane? Is it one of her mood swings? How will she ever fit into the Punjabi household again?

If the animals are not dying, are you?

The mood is morbid.

Mummy is taking it even more personally. She's questioning the Punjabi genes of the child. 'No Punjabi refuses meat.' I think she's suspicious of who the father is!

Then she turns to me in the evening and says gently, 'You know, most Punjabi women are vegetarians. So it must be a girl.'

She is now satisfied with her theory. I'm satisfied about not needing to see chicken again.

Ramit

Mummy keeps asking me about the chicken. Too much salt? Too much mirchi? Too less of something? Why isn't Mona eating her chicken?

Mona

Got a hush-hush call from my mom today.

'Ramit told me you haven't been eating chicken,' she whispered.

Uff, this Ramit!

'I don't know. There's this metallic taste in my mouth …'

'It must be the chicken your mother-in-law is making.' Clearly, Mom has made up her mind about what, or who, the problem is. 'She doesn't know our taste buds. You don't worry! I will get there and make you some delectable dishes! Hang in there, okay?'

I don't get a chance to defend Mummy's cooking before she hangs up.

Ramit

Poor Mona has been stuck in the bedroom. She hardly gets to leave it.

Got her some books of the non-pregnancy variety. Also some perfume to help with her olfactory issues.

Mona

That was a rather sweet gesture, but the minute Ramit left for work, I had to toss the perfumes out. The smell's too strong for me.

I may be giving birth to some sort of sniffer dog!

Ramit

Woke up with a start – it sounded like Mummy was moving furniture in the middle of the night, but the sheepish grin from my dearest wife made me realize it wasn't that type of noise.

From now on, we will be sleeping under separate blankets.

As it is, we haven't done anything in over three months.

Maybe I can unsubscribe from our LPG connection. Or get a bunch of balloons. Or open a stepney repair shop. My wife is producing so much natural gas, I could become a millionaire.

Mona

Today I farted in front of my mother-in-law.

And with that, the last vestige of my pride flew out of the window.

Week 12

A nuchal translucency scan helps detect the risk of
genetic issues with the foetus

Ramit

This is what nightmares are made of. Having your mother and mother-in-law under the same roof.

Mona's Mom arrived this morning and Mummy leaves tonight. There was a bit of a catfight about who would accompany us to the doctor, but then I managed to dissuade both of them.

Mona

Caught Ramit sweating it out as the two mothers came face-to-face.

Don't know why my Mom has decided to become the national flag of India in her saffron kurta, green salwar and unmatched white dupatta. I should get Shania to have a chat with her. Her dress sense is getting more and more atrocious by the day.

But I'm too worried to bother right now.

It's an important scan today. And I've never been more scared.

I can hear every piece of advice that's been thrown at me about *jaldi baccha karo*, biological clock etc., etc. Apparently the older the mother, the more the chances of the child having Down's syndrome, which is what we're checking for today. Something called an NT scan.

Ramit is being all don't-you-worry but I can see that frown on his face as he drives.

Ramit

Can't concentrate on driving. Panicking about the mothers. I can literally hear their voices in my head, arguing over who should look after Mona and the baby and why one's methods are superior to the other's. Just like they did at our wedding.

Wonder which of the two will murder the other first.

My money's on Mummy.

Mona

We've changed the ultrasound clinic. I'm not going to get an internal examination done again. I read up everywhere and you don't need to have that thing shoved up you to see the baby. So goodbye, Shahnaz Husain and hello Dr Rama Rathore.

Only Dr Rama Rathore turned out to be Dr *Ram* Rathore. Shit.

Ramit

For a minute, I thought my wife was about to pull her pants down in front of that man.

Mona

Dr Ram Rathore assuaged our fears by telling us that it'd definitely be an external scan, and then placed lots of goop on my stomach and moved the thing around. Colour returned to Ramit's face.

Ramit

The screen lit up, but I was worried about having that man's hairy knuckles on my wife's stomach. He was staring at his screen but I was watching his hand.

I tried to catch Mona's eye but she was gaping at the screen. I turned to see it too.

Mona

Is this thing actually inside me?

Ramit was shaking his head in disbelief. It was an outline of a real baby. I could actually see the baby. Our baby. A real baby. Not a blob. A *baby*.

Ramit saw it too, and he was beaming down at me so I quickly forced myself to smile back at him. Didn't want him to know how awkward it felt to have a baby, a human being, growing inside me.

I miss the blob. Where's the blob?

Oh my God! Am I not supposed to be overflowing with maternal feelings, all warm and fuzzy? I know I'm pregnant, but this is like there's something *inside* me. Which is what pregnancy means but ... where is the blob?

Ramit

It's a funny baby. Kept floating around as the doctor made notes of random numbers on the screen. Couldn't wipe the silly smile off my face. I held Mona's hand. It was a little shaky.

Then Dr Rathore started measuring the nasal bone and some thigh bone while taking us through the kidney and stomach and it was all so exciting.

He told us all was well after half an hour of pushing around. Then asked if we wanted to hear the heartbeat.

Mona

And then, suddenly, there was a magical drumming from within me.

And that's when I felt it. I felt a little ball of joy rolling in my stomach. I felt my eyes sting and I grinned at Ramit, who was grinning back at me, his ears pink with happiness.

'And this is the sound of the blood ...'

Ramit

Never thought 'whoosh whoosh whoosh' could sound so beautiful.

It was a special moment for us. A defining point in our relationship. An image of Mona smiling at me in college, her saying yes when I asked her to marry me, sitting down next to me at the pheras, opening the door for me when I got home for the first time ... all of it played in my head. And now, we are going to have a baby.

I held her hand in both of mine and we gazed at the screen like two lovers. Which we are.

Mona

We drove home holding hands, in silence. Actually, Ramit hasn't been able to let go of my hand since the scan. Every now and then he turns to smile at me and I know he's as happy as I am.

For years I've wondered why people had honeymoon babies. I guess I know now.

Ramit

When I pulled into the driveway, I saw the two mothers from the window, seated at the dining table, anxious, checking their phones, drinking their tea. Damn. Had forgotten all about them.

They rushed to us when we entered and Mona told them everything was fine.

The mothers clapped their hands and even hugged each other in relief.

I suggested we could finally tell people.

And then it began. The never-ending family drama.

'Wait another week,' Mona's mom said pointedly, a diplomatic smile on her face. 'What's the point of telling extended family immediately?'

A puff of smoke seemed to escape my mother's nose. I braced myself for the inevitable fight.

Mona

My heart sank to my toes. I knew my mother was talking about the hazaar Deols.

'We don't have the concept of *extended* family,' Mummy said indignantly. 'They are all well-wishers and once I tell the Deol family, they will only pray for Mona's good health.' Clearly they weren't considered well-wishers in the first three months.

'I'm not asking you to deny it when someone asks, but no point going around making a loudspeaker announcement.' Mom argued with her chin turned up, refusing to meet Mummy's seething eyes. What did my bechari-dressed-up-like-a-national-flag mother think she was doing, taking on my ex-school-principal mother-in-law?

'Besides, it's Mona and Ramit's big announcement,' Mom continued, not knowing how much of her own and our lives she was putting at risk by continuing with this argument. 'They should figure it out themselves. What do you guys think?' Both the mothers looked at us expectantly, piercingly, but I'd decided to do a PhD on the floor tiles.

We stood around in silence for a bit, till Ramit finally cleared his throat and announced he was going to call Dr Khan's clinic for an appointment to discuss the NT scan.

Both the mothers turned to Ramit in horror.

'Dr Who?' the mothers ask in unison.

'Dr Mehak Khan. The gyna…

'You're going to a Mohameddan doctor?' Mummy asked, aghast.

'You didn't tell me!' Mom shouted.

This was followed by a series of shocked protests. Ramit's ears went from pink to maroon.

Ramit

The inevitable fight has begun, but it's not between them, it's between team Mothers and team Pregnant Us.

Of all the things the mothers could be worried about, they've picked the faith of the doctor delivering Mona's ... I mean, our baby.

Spent an hour arguing with them on why it doesn't even matter.

'She won't let us swaddle the baby in Guruji's cloth from the Gurdwara,' Mummy argued.

I reasoned with her that Dr Khan delivers many children of different-faith parents and won't have an issue with it.

'She won't let us write Om on the baby's tongue with honey,' Mona's Mom adds. Mona's mother is an atheist. They don't even have an idol in their house. On Diwali they play bhajans off Shania's iPod. She wants to write Om on our baby's tongue? Who is she kidding!

'Mom, we shouldn't be giving the baby honey so early on in any case,' Mona said bravely.

'See? She's already brainwashing you!' Mummy jumped in to defend Mona's mother.

'You're so non-religious anyway, Mom. How does it even matter!' Mona snapped.

'Mona! How can you even say that! We have to give a newborn baby honey! What has this *doctor* been telling you?'

'She hasn't told me anything! I read it online! And in all the pregnancy books!' Mona looked at her mother angrily.

'Bade Papa goes to Dr Shafiq for his heart condition,' I told my mother pointedly. 'He's Muslim.'

'That's different! Other Muslim doctors are fine. But this is a brand new life! We can't have a Muslim doctor pulling out our child!'

Mona

I cannot believe this is happening! Ramit and I are just feeling more and more shocked at the absurdity of our mothers. It went on for an hour and five minutes.

I got very upset and called Dad to complain about Mom.

'Yaar, you know how it is with your mother. She must be worried about a Muslim doctor circumcising the baby. Just get her a glass of wine ...'

Turns out Dad was right. Both the mums had the same concern. Unleashed a speech that had them embarrassed to their toes. How dare they judge a doctor by her faith! How can they think someone so professional would do something like this? How can they be so irrational? They both looked guilty and sheepish. Then showed them some articles on the internet and a picture of her.

'So young?' my mom said, pulling the laptop towards her. 'How will she do your delivery? In my time ...'

Sigh!

Ramit

Finally, some peace. At least, a bit of peace. Mummy is on her way back, and now there are just two crazy women to deal with.

Mona

Now with the drama behind me, I'm wondering how to tell my friends.

Should I be a little dramatic and send them a picture of the ultrasound on the group? Or should I text each of them individually with some personalized message? Or should I say 'Coming soon: Baby Deol, September 7th!' Or does that sound too much like a Bobby Deol relaunch.

Or maybe I'll just walk into one of the get-togethers I have been avoiding of late, and announce it right before someone is about to cut a cake or something, and steal the limelight. Or I could invite them over for lunch and announce it then.

And to Laila Sachdev, I can simply say, oh, you're eight weeks along? I just found out I'm three months. Or will that make me sound like a bimbo who doesn't realize she hasn't had her period in three months?

I turned to Ramit and asked him how he was planning to tell his friends.

Ramit

I have to tell my friends? Won't that just make them picture us having sex?

Mona

Composed a simple text and sent it out. Flooded with replies.

Before I slept, saw Ramit on his phone. I'm guessing he was sending out messages to his friends.

Ramit

Trying to get some work done but the bheed is spamming me with congratulations.

Mona

Ramit's WhatsApp has crashed, courtesy his cousins flooding his inbox. He left the house grumbling.

And thanks to the mothers, all the relatives know. So much for being selective.

Got several strange phone calls including:

'I knew last Diwali only!' Somesh tayiji. That was six months ago.

'*Mubarak ho! Ladka ho!*' Cousin Teena, the sexist!

'Oh Thank God! I had been praying for so many years!' Ramit's dadi. Oh boy!

'My Roshan finally has a playmate!' Roshini. That child seriously needs some toys.

'Beta, second trimester is most dangerous. You need to take bed rest.' Paranoid Suhani bua from Doon. More like Paranoid Suhani bua from doom, as Shania calls her. I need to avoid all calls from her in the future.

Speaking of Shania: 'Oh, all's clear? Congrats again. And di, could you transfer 20K to me? I'll return it ASAP, I promise! And don't tell Mom-Dad please!'

Week 13

Your baby is now about the size of a peach

Mona

Mom is a peach. Okay, she also looks like a peach today, in that strange orange-and-red outfit, complete with a green rubberband around her ponytail. But she's also a peach for marching straight into the kitchen to attend to her daughter's needs.

She's confidently saying that the Punjabis don't know how to make chicken and she, who has grown up with a Christian best friend from Romania, knows how to make proper chicken, and immediately makes me a massive chicken pie.

Ramit

The chicken was so delicious, I was waiting for Mona to pass on her share of it, as always.

But she was wolfing it down like nobody's business.

It's true: A girl needs her mother. That's what I've learnt.

If Mummy was to see how Mona is having a go at her mother's food, she would've taken great offence.

157

Mona

Mom sat there, basking in pride as I asked for my third helping.

Then she brought out a basket of fried potato wedges and I scraped them off.

Then she brought out bread pudding, dripping with sweet mixed-fruit jam and butter and I had two helpings of that.

Basically, my taste buds seem to be returning to normal.

And another normal – since Mummy is gone, I am no longer under house arrest. So this afternoon, Mom asked me to walk with her to the vegetable shop right outside the complex. Apparently now that I'm three months along, I can get out of bed. I was so happy I skipped all the way. It was nice to be out in the March sun, and I forgot I was pregnant for a bit.

Then a car pulled up next to us and Laila Sachdev flung herself out of it and flung out what she'd eaten for lunch too.

I gave her a bottle of water and she thanked me and walked back with us.

Apparently she's been puking away every other day and has been feeling rather weak. I actually saw a tiny, really tiny, baby bump too. Mom glared at me for denying her the puking.

But she also turned it into an opportunity to boast. 'Oh, our Mona didn't have any puking!' she boasted. My innocent mother is quite competitive deep inside.

Laila turned to me questioningly and I blushed.

'I'm thirteen weeks now,' I told her.

She squealed and hugged me. She made some comments on how it would be wonderful to be on this journey together and how she wished I had told her earlier and how exciting that the kids would be around the same age and all that fake jazz.

Laila Sachdev and I stood at the gate chatting for a bit after that … more like she chatted and I nodded. She went on about how exciting it is and how she hasn't got a dating scan done since her doctor, at the very posh Mother L'Enfant Hospital, doesn't think it's necessary and how she really hopes it's a baby girl and how she's been working away and travelling but feels quite sick most of the time and how she gets terrible cravings and one day had wandered off to KFC at 10.30 a.m., before the store had opened, and asked for chicken popcorn.

How completely opposite her experience has been to mine. Also, she is a terrible exaggerator. There is no such thing as craving. I'm sure it's just her way of squeezing more attention out of the husband.

Then Mom walked out and interrupted us.

'It's your mother-in-law on the line for you, Mona. She said you're not answering your phone and she got worried.'

'Oh that's why you've had your mums over!' Laila realized finally. 'Lucky you.'

Ha! She should try having two crazy mums over!

'Where are your parents?' Mom, ever inquisitive, asked.

'They're in Singapore. I'm sure they'll visit soon.'

I saw a flicker of something in her eyes. Don't know what. 'And Shashi's family?' I asked.

Laila smiled a little … uncomfortably? 'They stay in Mumbai.'

Ha! She doesn't get along with her in-laws. I knew it!

'Well,' Mom said, being all altruistic. 'We are like your parents. Come over whenever you like. In fact, come over this weekend. I'll cook the two pregnant women a nice nutritious meal.' Gosh, my self-proclaimed MasterChef mother! I could see her planning the meal in her head already!

Laila agreed and a date was set.

Ramit

Mona sent me a text saying she's craving Nutties.

I searched all of Gurgaon for them and perhaps contributed to their only sale in years. When I got home, Mona was sulking.

She wouldn't tell me why.

Women!

Pregnant women!

Mona

I sent him that text at three in the afternoon. I may have died of my craving but no, he still decides to wait till evening.

Men!

They have no understanding of pregnant women!

What if I actually had a craving and this wasn't just a test of his love for me?

Ramit

The thing about mothers is that while they're nosy and intrusive and bully you around, they're also almost always significantly better cooks than your wife.

We were at the table, enjoying the lavish spread, when a lady wearing a red sari with a snake around her neck sauntered into our living room.

Yes. A snake. Around her neck.

Shania.

Mona

Mom was so horrified she shrieked, and Laila and Shashi Sachdev stood up to attack the intruder, but Ramit had the situation under control as Shania broke out into hysterical giggles, claiming she only wanted to see Mom's reaction to the snake. I told her that simply seeing her dressed in a sari had that effect and nobody had noticed the fake snake in the first place.

And then she blinked at me and said: 'Di, Shantanu isn't fake.'

And just like that, a slimy, slithery, disgusting black snake was released into my arms.

Ramit

If Mona has to deal with the crazy 500-member Deol khandaan, I have one Shania. And that's enough.

With everyone going ballistic and the crazy sister-in-law insisting that the snake had been de-fanged and that the pet was here to stay and with the mother-in-law fluctuating between bouts of anger and self-pity, I had to figure out what to do with the slithering reptile. I went hunting for a large cardboard box, using a bowl of milk as bait – that's what they do in the movies – and tried to lure the snake into the box.

Then it dawned on me that no way had that snake come on a flight from Pune, to which Shania replied that she bought it from a snake farm in Mehrauli, run by a dear friend who, by the sound of it, seemed dearer than just dear. And it cost her five grand. Cost me, to be precise, as I had sent her the last instalment of extortion money.

I would have picked a fight, but I had to run behind the snake with a box and a bowl of milk.

Mona

As Mom stormed off to call Dad and get him to talk some sense into his beloved daughter, and Ramit phoned people to find someone who could get this snake off our hands, I hissed at Shania.

'Shantanu! How can you name the snake Shantanu! He was your first boyfriend.'

'And I'm still very bitter about how he left me, so now Shantanu is mine for life. And you better tell jeej that ... Oh hellooooo ... I'm so rude, as is my family, to not have introduced us. I'm Shania.'

That's when I realized the Sachdevs were still there and that Shania had spotted Shashi Sachdev. I swear to God she adjusted her sari palla to reveal one boob and more of her cleavage.

I hurried by her side before she went any further, and quickly said, 'I'm so sorry. Shashi, this is my little sister, Shania. Shania, this is our neighbour Shashi and this is Laila, his *wife*.' I had to physically hold Shania's shoulders and turn her towards Laila, who was standing exactly half an inch away from Shashi but Shania had pretended she was invisible.

And for once I saw Shania's eyes light up at someone of the same sex. She gasped.

'Gosh! I absolutely love what you're wearing,' she said, rudely checking out Laila's gorgeous floral floor-length cotton dress.

'That's very kind of you,' Laila said politely. 'I like your sari too.'

'Oh yes. There's this quaint but absolutely beautiful sari shop in Pune. I bought a whole collection from them. I was at the Mohita Ashram, by the way – Om Shanti Peace Peace Shanti, such an enriching experience – and while I was able to give up all these worldly things, saris are my weakness!' She batted her eyelashes at them.

She has never worn a sari in the past twenty-eight years! Probably once she discovered how revealing and sexy all these new-age blouses could be...

'So, is this ashram for meditation or yoga or...?' It was amazing how Laila could sound so genuinely interested in someone as flaky as my sister. It takes one to know one, I guess.

'It's for this and that.' Oh good God, Shania clearly had no idea. I wonder which boy she had followed into the camp. She gasped again and grabbed Laila's perfectly manicured hand – changing the topic, I supposed. 'This nailpaint! I've been looking for something like this forever!'

'Do you like it? It's our company's new matt range that we're just starting to test market.'

'I love it! It's so gorgeous!'

Given up all worldly things, my ass!

'Which company is this?' Shania asked.

'Sparq. This will be in our Touch range.'

Shania gasped again. She could pass off as an asthma patient with all her gushing. And she was genuinely interested in Laila Sachdev. She hadn't even glanced at Shashi Sachdev again, and that's saying something!

'Shania, I want to speak to you right now!' my mother snapped.

'Not now, Mom.'

'NOW!'

'Mom!'

'NOW!'

Shania sighed and followed my mother inside obediently.

'And why are you dressed like you're headed for a funeral again?' I heard Shania ask my mother as they disappeared. I noticed my mother's clashing ensemble of black and grey salwar-kameez for the first time this evening and reluctantly agreed with Shania.

And then Ramit stood up, his hair plastered all over his forehead, his glasses askew, having been on all fours all this while trying to capture the snake and making 'breathing holes' in the box. We both turned guiltily to our guests.

'So … dessert?'

Week 14

By now, your waistline may have begun
to look a little thicker

Ramit

Without being rude, I decided to tell Mona to go shopping with her Mom before she left. Her boobs have continued to get bigger, and despite the million scarves Mummy had bought her, she definitely needed some new clothes.

Mona

As a part of a 'cleansing' exercise she learnt at the ashram, Shania has decided to 'take' us shopping. We will be paying, of course. But she'll be providing us with selfless, true advice. And it will be a test of her patience, as she will not buy anything for herself. She's dressed in a sheer blue sari. I think she simply wants to step out to show off her sari collection and her ample cleavage.

Now, I know for a fact that someone needs to take my mother to the market and teach her how to match outfits and tell her wearing pink slippers with a neon green suit is not the brightest of ideas, but then Shania said I need to buy myself some stylish maternity pants too – the kind with waistbands that cover the belly; Laila Sachdev told her about them.

Apparently, Laila Sachdev and Shania are now picket-fence buddies and catch up every day when she returns from work.

Shania maintains that if she ever gets out of this I'm-one-with-the-universe phase, which I'm sure will be very soon, she will turn to diva Laila for guidance on how to re-enter the fashion world.

Anyway, we got delayed going to the market because Mom was yelling at Shania for making fun of her polka-dotted salwar while she herself was dressed in ridiculous clothes – a low-neck peasant-sleeved blouse with a transparent chiffon sari and my only Gucci designer sunglasses on her head like some 1970s Bollywood actress.

Ramit

I got a panicked call from Mummy saying I can't let Mona drive.

So there I was, taking the first half of the day off to drive three bickering ladies to the malls.

Mona sat in the back seat, muttering about how my mother had probably gotten CCTV cameras installed in our home, since she clearly knows everything about our lives. I think she's right.

We reached the mall and I left the women to shop while I found myself a café to work in. Two hours later, the ladies joined me and took over my laptop.

Apparently they had spent three hours in the mall looking for maternity clothes, before realizing that their best option was to shop online. Which they could have done from the house as well.

A complete waste of a day.

Mona

So I've ordered four maternity slacks and these large kurtis but Laila Sachdev is walking around in skimpy dresses showing off her bump! It's apparently fashionable.

My sister has invited her to tea and plans are being made to meet Tina Tej Mushran as well. How has my yogi sister gained entry into their elite world?

Ramit was grumbling about his wasted day and how expensive all these maternity clothes are, when Laila walked in and laughed.

'You think the clothes expensive? Have you any idea what will happen when the baby comes? Do you know how much a pram costs? Or a cot? Or a car seat? Or high chair? Or a breast pump?'

And Ramit's ears turned crimson again! My husband is such a prude!

Ramit

Told Mona we're not getting a pram. My mum carried me around everywhere. That's how mothers and babies bond.

I should have said parents and babies. But it was too late.

I'm being made to sleep on the couch.

Week 15

Pregnancy hormones improve the appearance of your skin, giving you that special pregnancy glow

Mona

We're back in Amritsar for Holi. And I'm back on bed rest.

Everyone considers this a 'precious' pregnancy, since it's come around so late. All the attention is off the puking-in-the-fifth-month Mohini and turned on the miraculously-pregnant Mona.

Multiple relatives have come into the room to compliment my 'fair' skin, and Dadi also nodded her approval of my looks and pronounced I'm having a baby girl.

A Deol debate ensued.

Nishi bua said it's a boy, judging by the roundness of the belly. If it was a girl, apparently my belly would have been oblong.

Daisy chachi said it's a girl because women glow when they're carrying girls and turn ugly if they are carrying boys. She stole a rather obvious glance at Mohini, who looked half dead from all the puking.

Roshini, the one who is desperately looking for a playmate for her son, said it's a boy because I haven't puked at all – just like she hadn't. Eyes turned to Mohini again.

Vishi bua skyped from America and declared that it's certainly a girl because my hair is looking thicker.

Chiku, no-action-on-honeymoon, said I'm carrying twins, given the weight I've put on. There were multiple nods at that, till Mummy informed them that the ultrasound had shown only one child.

And Suttu wanted to do the ring test over my belly to figure out for sure.

Mummy, after she huddled out all the members of the family, asked me to lie down. And then she lifted my T-shirt – much to my horror – and said that since the line joining the navel to my pelvic area is crooked, it's a boy.

She then instructed me to put my feet up while she fetched me some more fruit.

Ramit

Was playing cricket in the driveway when I saw Mummy taking up yet another glass of orange juice for Mona. I won't be surprised if our child comes out looking like a damn orange.

Mona

Mom phones me from Doon to tell me Shania's yogi phase hasn't ended. But it's more about the skimpy blouses than spirituality. She is disgusted, but Dad refuses to look beyond the tip of his paintbrush. She's told me to do something about my sister when Shania comes for her 'turn' next week once we're back.

I told her about the gender debate I've sparked off. She informed me that the glow was from all the orange juice and fruits. Nothing else.

She thinks it's a boy because Ramit is the only child and he's a boy, and it always goes on the boy's side of the family, just like Mom had two girls because Dad has two elder sisters.

Who needs foetal sex testing in India when you have relatives?

Ramit

Shania was FaceTiming with us when she proclaimed loudly, 'You know why you're glowing, right?'

Mona exasperatedly asked about her theory. Shania helpfully explained that it was after-sex glow, since now we were in the safer phase of pregnancy and didn't have to … er … refrain.

I left them both at it and could hear Mona scolding her.

So glad I'm a single child.

Week 16

Sometime during the second trimester, couples may feel an increased interest in sex

Mona

I can always rely on Shania to botch things up. But this time it's been a welcome mess. She booked her tickets from Dehradun on the wrong date and this being the long Easter weekend, she is unable to get train tickets to Delhi. She won't take the bus because road journeys make her sick.

Which means, after many months, Ramit and I are alone again!

Ramit

American TV is full of lies. A pregnant woman's hormones do not go on overdrive.

Mona and I are sleeping on our king-size bed but Mona and her growing belly would rather nestle against the heap of pillows instead of me.

Mona

It's just so freaking hot!

Ramit is curled up in the Jaipuri while I'm in tiny cotton shorts and I'm still sweating away like a pig.

Now Ramit is ranting away about the electricity bill and suggesting I move to Antarctica.

My husband wants me to move to the South Pole while there are other husbands like Milind-Shashi who take their pregnant wives on a 'babymoon' to Paris.

What the hell is a babymoon?

Ramit

The Sachdevs have gone to Paris on a 'babymoon'. What the hell is a babymoon? Anyway, they should have taken Mona with them. Would have given me a few days to thaw. It's freezing in here.

Our only weekend alone in weeks, and we're sleeping in separate rooms.

Mona

I cannot believe how normal I'm feeling! When Mom told me I'll feel much better after the first trimester I hadn't believed her. But look at me now!

I even went for a walk and found Mrs Kapoor and Asha in the park.

'Achha, good news hai?' she said, eyeing my bulge.

Then she enquired after my stylish neighbour and I told her Laila was expecting too. I swear to God she looked jealous. Mr Kapoor may be in for some action!

When I got home, I switched on my laptop and scrolled through Facebook and imagined how I would announce the arrival of our baby. Maybe with a picture of me in the hospital with a bundle in my arms. It gave me goosebumps.

Then I thought, now that Laila Sachdev and I are friends, kind of, I should add her on Facebook. But I couldn't find her. Which was strange. Surely someone as stylish as Laila Sachdev had a Facebook account?

So I looked for her on LinkedIn. No trace.

So I searched for 'Sparq cosmetics + Laila'.

And there it was. Laila Haider, Marketing Head, Sparq Cosmetics.

Oh. Laila Haider. I found her on Facebook too. She had a stunning profile picture of herself on a cruise ship with the sunset in the background. And here Mom would never let me take a picture against the sunset as it brings bad luck as per *Qayamat se Qayamat tak* the movie. That's where my mom gets her superstition from!

Anyway, looks like Laila Haider hasn't changed her maiden name.

And I'm a bloody Deol!

Ramit

What on earth is she sulking about now?

Week 17

Pregnant women often have to deal with unwanted belly touching

Ramit

I have to fetch my sister-in-law from the station. Does no one use Uber any more?

It's Shania's turn to babysit my wife and I can imagine the destruction she'll leave behind.

Mona wanted to come with, but she was taking too long with her shower.

Mona

I was exhausted just holding the hand shower.

I've got myself a little plastic chair to sit on while washing my knees.

I also go through the daily ritual of discovering new things on my body everyday. The darkening line in the middle of my stomach. Bra marks and panty lines thanks to my expanding girth. The little red rash which I wouldn't have noticed otherwise but I hope now it isn't a reason to panic. Stretch marks.

And then after that exhausting shower, I reached out for the various vitamin E oils and creams I'm supposed to apply.

Mummy sent me a carton full of them from Amritsar. Mom immediately got competitive and sent me some natural oils from her friend's farm in Dehradun.

Obviously, both mums also gave full-on instructions on applying the smelly oils on my stomach, thighs, hips, butt, behind her knees, breasts and 'even the, you know, nipple area,' Ramit's Mummy had said in hushed tones. Good God! There have to be some boundaries, please!

And as I apply the oil in circular motions on my butt, as instructed, I break into – '*Main Jhandu balm hui Darling tere liye.*'

Ramit

Mona has been smelling like a parantha nowadays, so for once, I'm thankful for my sister-in-law. She turned up with some cocoa butter thing to replace Mona's disgusting oils.

She also did a great job pretending to gag and puke before handing it over.

Mona

I must admit it is better-smelling but … you know when it gets hot, and it gets hot a lot, I feel like the butter is melting and trickling down my back and my cleavage! It's yuck! Better-smelling yuck, but yuck indeed.

Ramit

Shania calls me at 8.00 p.m., asking to be picked up from some ashram in Kapashera. I was on my way back with two of my associates after a meeting.

After I picked her up, Vinay and Karanveer decided they didn't want to be dropped off at their drop-off points. Said they would just call a cab to my place and make things easier.

There was non-stop conversation in the car with Shania giggling and them turning pink with pleasure at all the attention. She was telling them all about ashram life and they mentioned quitting their 'dull' work to pursue that spiritual stuff. Yes, they said that in front of me, their boss. I made a mental note to mention this during their appraisals.

Then Shania asked them to stay for dinner.

Mona

My sister walked in wearing her see-through black chiffon sari and tube-top blouse, followed by two puppy-faced boys from Ramit's office. And one of them I'm sure is engaged. Doesn't she know I'm too pregnant to play hostess?

Ramit rolled his eyes at Shania and washed his hands off any blame for the unexpected guests. Shania was raiding Ramit's bar and ordering Lakshmibai to make extra rotis. I wondered about ordering something from Kadhai Mirch Ki, our local dhaba, but what did it matter? These boys were so taken by her, I could've fed them grass from our garden.

I'm asking Mom to call Shania back. If she's such a yogi, she should be meditating. All she does is check herself out in her saris before galloping off to ashram meetings and flirting with unsuspecting men.

At ten, when we finally opened the door to say goodbye to the boys, we found Laila Sachdev – sorry, Haider – standing at the door in a lovely pink dress, not looking pregnant at all.

It was the boys' lucky evening.

Week 18

Not all the weight you're gaining is your baby. Your breasts may be growing bigger and your blood volume is still increasing

Mona

Shania accompanied me to Dr Khan's clinic since Ramit had some investor meeting. We were in the waiting room when Shania pulled down her sunglasses to ogle at all the pregnant women.

'They're bloody stylish, this lot!' she whispered to me. 'Why can't you be like them?'

'For starters, they're a whole lot thinner.' I ran through a series of expletives in my head, but answered calmly. I was the dignified older sister, after all.

They made me stand on the weighing machine and Shania gasped. I made a mental note to book her on the earliest train back to Doon.

'Eight kgs up!' the assistant said, making a note.

I wanted to tell her that each of my breasts probably weighed four kgs. Plus, I'm supposed to have a lot more blood in my body now. It's not all fat!

Ramit

Cousin Swaroop landed in Delhi. Received a WhatsApp message on the group saying he wanted to meet all the bheed tomorrow night. Just as I was typing out a message about it being too short a notice and Mona and I would be busy, Mona promptly responded with a 'looking forward' text and went on to actively suggest places we could meet at.

She's that desperate for food.

Mona

I mean, why not. Everyone tells me I should eat guilt-free!

Except Dr Mehak, who said I have exceeded my weight-gain quota. But my next appointment is after four weeks and I'm going to be more regular with my walks and lose some of that water retention by then.

Ramit

So we went to this place which serves thaalis and typically Mona and I would share one. But today she wolfed down not one or two but five of their lachha paranthas and was the last one to finish eating.

And people were egging her on!

'*Achhe se kha, Mona. Yahi toh time hai.*'

I wanted to say that there were twenty weeks more to go, but Mona looked so happy with the bheed for a change. I couldn't ruin it.

I'm just glad it was fixed-price thaali.

Mona

Such great food! What a wonderful evening! I say as much to Ramit.

Ramit

Lovely evening with the bheed? Crazy pregnant woman…

Mona

Can you believe that? Laila Sachdev came over to say hello and ask how I was doing and then asked me if I had any of the caramel cake left over from when Mom was here. And when I laughed and said obviously not, she asked me if I could make her some or get her the recipe. Just look at her! Shamelessly asking me for food!

Says she's craving it.

Laila and her cravings! All attention-seeking behaviour, if you ask me. There's no such thing as cravings!

Ramit

Big fight. I suggested we ask Mona's mom to send us some caramel cake with Rani next week to pass on to Laila. She is pregnant, after all. But Mona burst into a string of expletives about how I'm so naïve I can't see through skinny Laila Sachdev's drama.

Mona

I found Shania curled up on the couch with Laila Sachdev. They're bonding big time. Laila is perpetually in our living room or Shania is perpetually there.

And listen to Shania's audacity! She was telling Laila, 'I've spoken to Mom. She'll send you the caramel cake next week, Laila.'

This Laila has the world wrapped around her little finger! She's just like my sister!

Ramit

Shania called me and asked to be picked up from some store in Greater Kailash. I was worried because Vinay and Karanveer were with me again. They stuck their head out of the car window as I went into the store and it was exactly like travelling with pet dogs.

Shania had the sales attendant tailing her, all red-faced and delighted to be spoken to. She had also charmed him into giving her a discount.

'Thank you,' she batted her lashes at the poor man. 'What did you say your name was?'

'Vik ... Vik ...' We never found out whether he was Vikram or Vikas or what.

Back in the car, she sent off my highly qualified premier institute MBA graduates scrambling over each other to fetch her a packet of cigarettes. I told her it was unbecoming of her ashram life, to which she gave me a pitiful look and said, 'Oh jeejs, how conservative of you! We at the ashram are a liberal lot, you know. Loosen up!'

Made me feel ancient and narrow-minded. From now on, I'm only minding my own business.

Mona

Shania is wearing this bright orange bikini blouse with her green chiffon sari, and going partying with some 'ashram' friends. Who is buying her these things? Ramit has nothing to say to her. He just shrugs and says, 'She's an adult, Mona. We can't be so conservative about her life choices. Loosen up!'

Loosen up? My sister has to get back to Doon at the earliest.

Week 19

The scan around the 18–20th week shows you an
almost fully formed baby

Ramit

We went back to Dr Ram Rathore's ultrasound room. Still not completely comfortable with his hand on her stomach.

'There you go. That's your baby. I'll now take you through all the measurements we'll be recording for this level-two scan.'

There was a face, a nose, somewhat creepy eye sockets, hands that flipped right from the head to below the bum in seconds, a really big foot, stomach and kidneys and bladder and lungs and heart and…

I think it's a boy.

Mona

So tiny! Minus the big foot.

But so pretty. Minus the eye sockets. Those were scary. Alien-like.

So delicate! Except the way it kept flipping.

It's a boy. It's definitely a boy. I wish there was some way I could ask.

Ramit

I asked. Told the doc I could see the ... er, you know.

That was when he laughed and said it was just the umbilical cord and not the penis.

Mona

Obviously our man's ears turned red at the P-word.

Ramit

Minus that bit, it was quite a morning. Wish we could see the baby every week.

Mona

Ramit got so excited by the ultrasound he took the day off and we went to the mall for lunch.

He insisted Dr Ram Rathore was trying to cover up for not being discreet about the body part and that it's actually a boy. I hope he's right; our daughter will never find shoes given the size of that foot we saw today.

Anyway, all was well till I stepped out of the mall and suddenly there were children pouring out of every corner. It's a weekday and there are still so many kids around.

And when we were at Big Chill, one poor mother was holding her baby on one hip and rocking him, and eating her food standing up. That's when the realization hit me. I'll never get to eat in peace again.

Ramit

For Mona, everything comes down to eating.

I decided to check my email and tune her out.

Mona

Ramit had nothing to say to me, as always, when I shared my feelings with him, so I turned back to the scene at the mall.

I watched mothers chase their children from one corner to another, bribe them with iPads, mobile phones. I saw mothers sighing loudly as their child threw a tantrum in the middle of the shop. I saw an embarrassed mother quickly stacking the clothes her child had pulled off the rack. I saw one woman, clearly in pain as her child pulled her hair while she tried to make a payment at the counter. What is with kids nowadays!

It's so disturbing, I decided to make a list of the things *my* child would definitely NOT do!

First, no tantrums. My child will be calm and I'll be calm, and she or he will never even interact with kids who throw tantrums.

I'm not going to coochie-coo with my kid either. No funny baby noises. How do they expect children to pick up a real language if they keep talking gibberish to them!

I'll just calmly talk to my baby and establish some sort of non-verbal code with it for when it's hungry. I'm pretty sure that's possible. I've read books on how one can decipher what each type of cry stands for. Mothers and babies are supposed to have that type of bond, you know.

I will not take my child to the movies till it learns to sit straight in the seat without kicking the *saamne wali* seat out of excitement. I hate that! Otherwise I'll just leave him/her behind with the nanny. Because of course, we'll have a nanny. A reliable, good nanny. Not a maid.

I will not carry my child everywhere. And I'll have the pram. Why do these parents pull a wailing child out of the pram and rock them and carry them around the mall? They're spoiling them. They just need to train their kid from the start.

I will also not have a snotty child. He will learn to wipe his own nose just as soon as his toilet training is done, which will be when he's four months old. They say you should toilet train your baby the moment they starts sitting.

My child will be multilingual and have a polished accent. They say babies can pick up multiple languages very early on. I'll just buy those French- and Spanish-teaching CDs and that should be enough. '*Baa Baa Black Sheep*' in French.

My child will not mispronounce. It's not cute! I'm very particular about language, you see.

My child will be super-cheerful and not hide behind me in front of strangers. I don't want my baby to become clingy.

And I won't be cleaning up all the time after my child is done playing. We Indians pamper our children too much. They don't do this abroad. I've never seen it in the movies.

And my kid will never cry on flights. Neither Ramit nor I have any issues with flying so why should our kid?

Ramit

I don't know what Mona is writing down in her little notepad but she suddenly turns to me and says, 'Next time you fly, I want you to pick up as many air sickness bags from the flight as you can.'

Mona

That should sort it out. A puke bag in the car, one in my purse, one in the baby bag, one in each room of the house. No messes that way. It's sensible to start collecting these things early, no?

And diapers. I will always have tons of disposable diapers.

I wonder how much space they take? Can't be too much. I mean, sometimes I carry two Whisper Ultras in my bag, and that's fine. We won't need more than two diapers, right? All these companies advertise all-night-dry diapers, so they should last twelve hours, right?

By way of conversation, I discuss my aspirations for my child with my mom over the phone. She guffaws like she has never guffawed before. Between fits of laughter, she says, 'If it were only that easy, Mona.' Then she tells me they used cloth nappies for us, so that's what I'll need. Not diapers promising twelve-hour protection.

'And no baby language? Do you know you couldn't say doggy till you were five? You would say dojjie. And you couldn't pronounce 'th'. You said 'dh'. So you would walk around saying 'dhat dojjie is dhere, dhat dhojjie does dhat.' It was so cute! It's so cute when kids mispronounce stuff! Why would you not want that in your child?'

Well, dojjie does sound cute.

Week 20

By now, you might feel the baby moving, though the senstation is so slight, it can be written off as gas

Mona

Ran into Laila Sachdev sporting her baby belly and wearing these stylish yoga pants and a ganji top. She announced she was off to yoga. Yoga! I asked her if it's safe and she said, of course. It's prenatal yoga, it's amazing, had I not heard of it? I laughed a little too loudly to cover up and said, of course I *knew,* and I'd thought she meant regular yoga and that wouldn't be safe, would it? To which she studied me curiously for a moment and asked if I'd like to join. Said there's some lady who holds classes just around the corner and it would be so nice to do something together. Next thing you know she'll ask us to sign up for antenatal classes together! I told her I'll give it a think and that I'm pretty active with my walks. She doesn't need to know it's only once a fortnight.

Then she asked me how everything was coming along.

I told her all about my scan and she said she had had it done yesterday too. Show off!

But then she asked if the baby has been kicking. Hers apparently has.

Now I know she's just an exaggerator. How can she, a good four weeks behind me, feel the kicks when I can't!

Ramit

I read aloud from Google: 'If you lie down still, you can feel it. It's like popcorn popping. It's like little butterflies fluttering. It could also feel like gas.'

Asked Mona to lie down, relax and concentrate.

She's getting so competitive! She really wants to feel those movements now that Laila's felt them.

I asked if she could feel the butterflies when she lay down.

'Ummm … No. It feels like gas,' she said at last.

'No, no! You've got it wrong. It must be the baby,' I encouraged her.

'Give it a minute and your nose will tell you it was gas!' she snapped.

Okay, so it was gas.

'Concentrate,' I egged her on after a bit. 'Maybe you'll feel a little bit of popcorn?'

She lay quiet for a moment and said softly, 'Ramit…'

'Yes?' I said excitedly.

'I feel like having caramel popcorn.'

Mona

Today I thought I would faint. I've put on one kilo in one week. At this rate, I'll have added twenty more kilos by the end of this pregnancy. And that's if I don't put on 1.5 kilos a week like Mohini has been doing in Amritsar.

I sulked for a while.

I'll just starve myself, no eating out, start exercising, real exercising rather than the stroll in the park…

So I joined that prenatal yoga class after all, and there I was, wobbling inside while Laila practically glided in like a ballerina.

'Hello, Mona. I'm Jaishree, your instructor. How're you doing?'

'I'm fine,' I said, shaking her hand.

'Nearing the end now of the pregnancy?'

'Umm … I'm five months…'

'Oh.' She was obviously eyeing my weight. 'Great! Let's get started!'

We did all sorts of random exercises and stretching and my muscles began aching. I was questioning whether the poses were safe for pregnant women when she asked us to lie down flat on our backs and relax.

And that's when I felt it.

A kick. A real kick in my abdomen. That wasn't gas. That was definitely a kick!

Ramit

When I got home, Mona ran up to me and placed my hand on her belly.

'There, did you feel that?' she asked, excitedly.

'Umm … no.'

She looked disappointed and positioned my hand differently.

'That?'

'No.'

We waited.

'THERE! That one!' she said excitedly.

Couldn't feel a thing but I plastered on a fake smile and nodded and she happily continued to hold my hand over her stomach, looking delighted.

She's really so sweet.

Mona

It's like I'm giving birth to Bruce Lee. That's the amount of somersaulting and kicking this baby's been doing since the day I got back from yoga. Or maybe it always had and I had never really acknowledged it till now.

So exciting!

Week 21

The second trimester is often referred to as the golden trimester

Mona

So it's been established by now that Bollywood's totally off the track as far as the depiction of pregnancy goes.

But Hollywood movies aren't any less!

For starters, pregnant women in India don't wear heels, I don't know how it is abroad. Here you have a mother and a mother-in-law who watch you like a hawk if you do anything remotely fashionable. And imagine this comes from my mother, who has no fashion sense whatsoever! Meanwhile Laila Sachdev wears all these wedge heels and boots and…

Anyway, back to Hollywood.

Pregnant women in Hollywood have large tummies, but no butts and no saggy boobs. That's just so wrong! You expand everywhere. Especially the butt. Even Laila Sachdev's butt is growing. Ramit feigns disinterest when I ask him, and pretends he hasn't noticed her butt, but I have eyes at the back of my head, you know!

And then they always show these skinny pregnant women doing yoga! Stretches, surya namaskars and headstands! Let me tell you, prenatal yoga is nothing as glamorous. It's about deep breathing and holding your tummy and saying

213

'Om'. And, okay a little bit of wrist-bending and stretching. And okay, maybe some women can lift their legs in the tiger pose and be all cool like Laila Sachdev and, okay, the teacher claims some *can* do the headstand with a little practice, but for me, that is *not* happening.

Today when I lay down to do the shav aasan – best yoga aasan in the world – I started planning my babymoon.

Ramit

Not this babymoon business again!

And where am I going to find the money for it? I've just learnt my insurance doesn't cover maternity, can you believe that? And she wants a babymoon.

Mona

No babymoon it seems. I stormed out of the house on the pretext of my walk.

I'm sure I can drop all expectations of a baby shower too, in that case. But seriously, who's going to throw me a baby shower, anyway? The duelling mothers? Or Shania, who'll sit in a cloud of cigarette smoke chanting Om Shanti Shanti Peace Peace? I'm sure Tina Tej Mushran will throw a posh one for Laila Sachdev with all her posh caterers.

Was just thinking of Tina when she emerged from a Red SUV.

'Oh lovely! How pregnant you look!' She gave me a big hug and it cheered me up a bit, though now I'm wondering if it was really a compliment. I mean, I'm still in my fifth month.

Or maybe my sixth? I don't understand how these weeks correspond to months.

'How gorgeous is the dress!' Shania had made me buy this dress from Cotton Sombre's.

'Thank you.'

'How far along now?'

'I'm twenty-one weeks.'

'Ah! When I was pregnant the first time, I didn't show till the thirty-sixth week. I remember we'd gone partying and I met this dear college friend of mine, Ashok, the cardiologist in Sunshine Heart Institute? Dear, dear friend of mine, really. His wife and I had done a course in candle-making together. Anyway, we were at this party and dancing and he says, I hope I don't offend you but you've put on a bit of weight since we met last. I told him, Ashok! I'm six and a half kilos up! I'm pregnant!' She laughs fondly at her memory and I want to throttle her. 6.5 kgs! 'But during my second and third pregnancy, I showed much earlier. Like I had people making way for me in the elevators, and during Sameer's time, I put on thirteen kilos! Beat that!' I didn't want to tell her I already had.

Met Mrs Kapoor in the park after that. She looked at my dress rather disapprovingly. I'm sure she was the type who draped her dupatta around herself when she was pregnant so that no one ever got to know.

'Achha, dress pehni hai,' was all she had to say as little Asha climbed up the monkey bar.

I made small talk and she gossiped about her sister-in-law in America who had recently had a baby girl who was born at 2.8 kilos. I thought 2.8 was supposed to be good and said so to

her. She turned her nose up at me and said Asha was almost
four kilos when she was born!

'You have to eat well. Weight loss toh happens only later.'

I eyed her butt and seriously doubted her philosophy.

As I walked back some random aunty stopped me, smiling
and eyeing my belly. She then actually touched it. Here was a
woman I had never seen before in my life and she was happily
making physical contact!

'Koi good news?'

Thank God this time, the answer was yes.

Week 22

Naming a baby can be tricky. Making a list will help

Mona

My Dad's side of the family is basically nuts. Possibly that's the reason I rarely talk about them, or even acknowledge their existence. I believe Shania has gone totally on Dad's side of the family.

Anyway, Mom had dutifully broken the news about my pregnancy to Suhani bua about two months ago, and since then, by the clock, every Monday morning at 11 a.m., I've received a gloom-and-doom call from her.

'You are now in you twenty-second week, Mona.' She is my very own personal calendar. I should have simply employed her services during my ovulation time and we could have had this baby years ago!

'This week is very dangerous for you.' According to Suhani bua, every week is a very dangerous week for me. 'Your mother has assured me you're doing nothing strenuous but my friend's daughter-in-law...' And then she proceeds to narrate this horror story about of some distant acquaintance. Every single week. Every Monday morning.

My Dad's side of the family is basically nuts.

So to distract myself from this craziness, I've decided we need to start working on some baby names. We're midway through the pregnancy after all.

Ramit

I tried reasoning with Mona about getting the grandparents involved in this whole baby-naming business. I was named by my grandmother, so shouldn't we at least ask Mummy for suggestions? And then quickly added that Mom should suggest too.

Got late for work because the crazy pregnant lady blamed me for not being interested in the baby and wanting to brush off any responsibility whatsoever. I even suggested Mummy can name the baby if it's a boy, and Mom if it's a girl, to be fair.

Personally think Mona's worried about her own Mom's creativity. She hates her name. But I'm pretty all right by my Mummy's. I mean, she named me Ramit, not Amit. Which is good, right?

Mona

Letting the Deols name my child? No thanks! It's bad enough he'll have to carry their last name. I mean, nothing wrong with it but the Sunny Deol, Bobby Deol jokes just never end!

And who is Ramit trying to fool, talking about his family's creativity? Mummy's told me about the whole naming fiasco and this is how it goes.

His father's brothers are called Ramesh, Dinesh, Monish, Sudesh.

Then Ramesh married Somesh.

And they had Swaroop, Abhiroop, Dhoop.

Yes, Dhoop. Like agarbatti. The poor man keeps such a low profile, possibly because of his name.

And when the panditji had picked the letter R for Ramit, Dadi immediately suggested Roop to match Swaroop, Abhiroop and Dhoop; Mummy decided not to let her mother-in-law have the upper hand, and named him Ramit instead. So I will not let my mother-in-law have the upper hand either.

My own mother and father on the other hand, I can picture them cooing over my crib and saying:

'So Colonel, what should we name her?'

'Ah, Madhu, anything you want. Mona-Shona type will do. Who cares?'

I could be wrong, of course. Because Dad wasn't a colonel when I was born. He was a major. The rest of the conversation though, I will bet you it was exactly that.

Ramit

'Here's my list,' I told Mona, ready to impress her with how much I cared about *our* child!

Varun aka Vicky.

Aivaan aka Avi.

Chiragh aka Chiru.

Romair aka Romeo (cute, no?)

Tushar aka Tushy.

Purab aka Purab. Because if we call Purab Pur, it would sound like a fart, haha.

'Pur would be a fart but Tushy would mean nothing?' she snapped.

'Well...'

'And Aivaan? What does that even mean?' she threw her hands up in exasperation.

'It means ... something. I don't know. We can look it up.'

'Let me tell you what it means. It means Haivaan. Haivaan! The Devil! Monster!' she exploded, looking a bit like one herself.

Then she went on: 'And why do each of those options have nicknames? Why can't you *not* be a Deol for a change? And why doesn't your list have any girl names?'

'Because ... Well, what's on your list!' I didn't want to tell her I was still sure it was a penis in the scan and not an umbilical cord. The doctor hadn't fooled me.

She rolled her eyes dramatically, pretending to be disappointed in me as she picked up her list.

'Sameer, Aarav, Advay, Nishant, Rudraksh, Rahul...'

'And for a girl?' I interrupted.

'And if it's a girl, Avni.'

I waited for her to continue but she looked at her piece of paper nonchalantly.

'You fraud! You have only one girl name too,' I accused her.

She turned her nose up at me. 'I'm sorry! I didn't need options because Avni is such a beautiful name.'

'And what does Avni mean?'

'It means ... light.'

I whipped out my phone and Googled. 'It means earth,' I informed her.

'Maybe you're just looking at the wrong website,' Mona said dismissively, still not meeting my eye.

So I Googled 'Avni + light'.

'I can't find a single website listing that meaning.'

'Ramit, will you stop being so competitive and just decide if it works or not.'

'I'm the one being competitive?'

Mona

It continued for a good hour.

Our shortlist is Alina for a girl. And Kabir for a boy.

Yes, I know neither of the names was on anyone's shortlist earlier.

Ramit

Mummy has flipped over us having picked names without consulting panditji. Her exact words: '… without consulting me – err – panditji.'

Just because Dadi had forced her to consult the pandit.

I told her we're the parents and we don't believe in pandits, and how she knows I'm almost an atheist to which she shushed me and said I needed to lower my voice lest Dadi or Bade Papa or anyone else hear me, and I reminded her I'm in freaking Delhi and she's in freaking Amritsar, to which she shouted at me for using words like 'freaking' in front of my mother.

Mona

Mom suggested Laila for girl.

I'm not speaking to her again.

Week 23

You could be feeling a little off-balance, both physically
and emotionally

Mona

Waddling around, packing my XXL-sized clothes. Mom is livid I'm off to Amritsar again and not coming to Doon. She says Dad is missing me, but I seriously doubt he even looks up from his canvas to know I don't live in Dehradun any more.

I asked Mom to come with us to Amritsar but she got even more upset.

Then calmed down finally and asked if I wanted anything from Doon. What? Is she coming now? Is it her turn to babysit me?

'I used to have that gorgeous beige stole, remember, I wore so often to college? Get it with you.'

'Arre, I'm not coming right now. I can send it next week with Laila, if you like. She is coming, na.'

Sorry? How does she know Laila is going to Dehradun? And *why* is Laila going to Dehradun?

'Oh, she and Shania have been in touch. I'm so glad for her, Mona. Shania has finally broken off the yogi phase. Laila has got her interested in fashion designing and she spends a lot of her time in her room now. She's doing some course online. Being quite serious about it. And she was a decent artist in school. Maybe she'll do well. I'm so glad Laila's guiding her. She's like the older sister Shania never had.'

'Excuse me!'

'Oh, you know what I mean,' Mom said hurriedly. 'You're more friends than sisters, hehe.'

I told Mom if nothing she would herself benefit from Shania's fashion designing course. Then slammed the phone on her just as she slammed the phone on me.

Ramit

Mona's mother called to tell me that Mona's pregnancy hormones are acting up. As if I didn't know.

Mona

Am so glad we're going to Amritsar instead of Doon. At least people appreciate me here.

I was whisked from the station (wasn't allowed to fly because that would mean pressure, etc., according to Mummy) and planted on the sofa that I swear sank under my weight. I could feel the other side lift slightly off the ground.

Skinny Ramit sat on the chair opposite and buried himself in his phone as the relatives engulfed me with their questions.

Puking Mohini came in and we bumped our baby bumps and exchanged some morbid tales on acidity for a while, till she left to puke and I was allowed some rest.

Ramit

Mummy asked me why Mona was walking funny. I told her Mona had a stitch in her bum. Mummy was horrified and asked me when this surgery had happened. Told her a muscle pull is common during pregnancy as the uterus adds too much weight on the rest of the body.

I don't know why Mummy insists on asking me questions and then doesn't like me sounding knowledeable about anything. She huffed away saying she had been perfectly balanced and also had worked all nine months during her pregnancy, much to Dadi's dismay.

Mummy always takes great pride in telling us stories where she's put down her mother-in-law. Yet hates being put down as the mother-in-law.

Mona

Daisy chachi hounds me about Suttu's well-being. Asks me how often I see her, how she was looking the last time I saw her, and generally whines about her daughter being in Delhi while she's stuck in this terrible Amritsar. Then asks me to find Suttu a boy, given that she's nineteen already and will be finishing her fashion designing course next year. I want to tell her I have another wannabe fashion designer to take care of first, but don't say anything, then dutifully let her stuff my face with whatever laddu she thinks is best for me and the baby.

Mummy comes in shortly and sits down with the calendar to do some 'planning'. Thank God that word has a different meaning now.

Ramit

Mummy wants to decide on dates for the *mundan* and *naam karan* ceremony – dates for shaving and naming the baby. I tell her we'll be having neither of those because we don't believe in any of it.

She launches into a lecture on how disappointed she is in me and keeps looking at Mona for encouragement but Mona refuses to raise her eyes from the bowl of fruit someone's put in her lap.

Mona

Eventually Mummy returned to our room tearfully, holding a knitted jumpsuit for the baby and saying she had wanted to weave in the name before giving it to us, but now that there would be no naming ceremony, she sniffed … but Ramit kept staring at his phone.

Then…

Then she handed me another hand-knitted sweater and said, 'This is for your friend Laila's baby. It's so nice that you're going through your pregnancies together.'

Laila has obviously done some sort of black magic over everyone in my family!

Week 24

Around this time, your baby's taste buds start developing

Mona

Back home, after Suhani bua's weekly doomful call, I got a call from Ramit's Mummy:

'As per Google,' she said knowledgably, 'your baby can now taste what you're eating.'

Someone has clearly taught her how to use the internet to give us a harder time. She's obviously sick of Ramit putting her down with his Googled pregnancy knowledge.

'No, Mummy, I don't think it can taste what I'm eating. I think the taste buds are starting to develop but actual tasting doesn't happen till much later,' I explained gently.

'I think you should ask that doctor about it.'

'Her name's Dr Mehak.'

'That is a nice name. It's better than Alina.' She doesn't approve of our shortlist, clearly. 'Rina, Mina, Tina, Alina, so common, no?'

Because common names are not so common in the Deol family, right?

Then she sniffed pitifully. 'I know I'm *only* the grandmother, but have you considered the name Avni?'

Ramit

I had been looking forward to a sumptuous spread at the dining table today since Rani had arrived from Dehradun, but I found myself faced with lauki, tori and tinda.

Mona stared at her plate hatefully too.

'Apparently I'm supposed to eat this now,' she said dismally.

I walked to the kitchen and made myself a cheese sandwich. I'm not the one with a baby in my stomach. Uterus. I don't have a uterus. Whatever.

Mona

Ramit has been complaining non-stop about being faced with morbid, bland, nutritious food for three days. So to make a point, I asked Laila, who was over to say hello, how her vegetable guzzling is going. So that Ramit could see that pregnant women are supposed to eat healthy.

'Oh, terribly. I end up having boiled veggies all the time!' I looked over at Ramit, who refused to look up from his phone. 'But I don't want to put on too much weight so I am being careful, of course. Otherwise, there're so many nicer ways of having the veggies. I mean, vegetable lasagne, cream of broccoli soup, cheesy cauliflower...' Ramit then looked up with interest.

'But, I'm already four kilos up now,' she continued, 'and I have to be careful I don't put on more than eight or nine. So difficult to lose it later. So well, we're having the usual vegetables sautéd in soy sauce, vegetable pulaos, salt and pepper – grilled, not fried ... though sometimes I do cheat and have them fried in the air fryer. But Shashi doesn't mind it. He's always been good with veggies.'

'So there *are* better ways of eating veggies.' Ramit looked at me pointedly.

I ignored him. All I could think of was Laila saying she's four kgs up. Four kgs! I was four kgs up within a month!

Then Ramit stood up and poured himself a glass of wine, to which Laila said, 'Oh, do you have a red? I wouldn't mind a glass. I've had such a long day at work.'

Is she serious?

'Is it safe?' Ramit asked.

She laughed. 'Of course!' She looked over at me questioningly. 'Haven't you been drinking? A glass or two is okay, you know.'

I'm a behenji all over again.

Week 25

Friends and family may bombard you with advice on pregnancy and labour

Mona

Tina Tej Mushran is sitting cross-legged on my sofa again, holding an electric cigarette and blowing out puffs of smoke.

'Tej has warned me to stop. So here's to electric ones now. They taste nothing like the real thing. Nothing.'

Yet there she is, puffing away like a train engine. I still don't understand why she's planted herself in my living room.

'I was on my way to Anandita Dasgupta's art exhibition. She's such a dear friend of mine, so close. In fact, I was invited for her grandfather's ninetieth birthday only last week. If there's anyone who knows how to throw a party, it's darling Anandita. The catering … lip-smacking and how! And Laila, of course. She throws great parties too. Oh it was divine, what she did last year for Shashi's. It was his fortieth, you know. Too bad they went away to Maldives this year. I was hoping for a party. She was getting the same caterers as the ones at Akanksha Sarovar's engagement. Too bad that engagement broke up. Anyway, Andy's exhibition was just down the road so I thought I'd come see you too. How're you keeping, love?'

'I'm doing fine.'

She studies me critically and then exhales another electric puff.

'So, labour, huh?'

This seems to be quite a conversation starter.

Mrs Kapoor at the park also recently narrated all her gory stories about labour.

'Asha was born after seventeen hours of labour. And unlike these modern women, I didn't take an injection, you know. I was totally natural. Normal delivery. I was the first one to deliver normally on my entire in-laws' side. My mother-in-law gave me five tola gold. Has your mother-in-law told you what she'll be giving you?'

As if I needed a reward for popping out a child!

And then there are my own mother's stories!

'You were the more difficult one. I went in at 1 a.m., you arrived at 3 p.m. But Shania, she was quite easy. Two hours tops. Probably that's where the easiness ended with Shania. Mona, she told me yesterday she wants to get her belly button pierced. I've told her I've had it! Next thing you know she'll want a nipple pierced and...'

And the mother-in-law's stories:

'Ramit was a C-sec. Somesh bhabi's three children were C-sections too. Vishi toh almost died while giving birth to Swaroop. It's the size of his head, you know. Too large. It got stuck, they say. And Roshini, she shat on the labour table while pushing.'

Now I don't know how I'll ever look at Roshini's face without thinking of that story.

'Mine was so painful, don't ask,' Tina Tej says now. I haven't asked, of course.

'I took the epidural immediately, you know. I'm so bad with pain,' she says dramatically. 'I'd told my doc weeks in advance that the minute I break my water, I want the goddamn injection in me. Dr Shimauli, the same one Laila's going to? Very well known. So is Mehak, the one you're going to; I know her personally. She was the doctor for my close friend Mini Ahuja. You know her, right? Married to Vikas Ahuja of Le Torini Spa and Hotels? Anyway, Laila has been wanting to go the whole natural way. Says she's heard too many stories about backache and recovery issues with the epidural to try it. She thinks she's being brave. I think she's being bloody stupid. I told her, Laila, darling, I was twenty-four when I had my first one. You're thirty-eight.'

Laila is thirty-eight!

'Oh, you do know she's thirty-eight, right?' Tina says, judging my expression. 'That's right. And Shashi's forty-one. Not the youngest of parents. But then again, there are so many oldish parents now. And it's a first baby for both of them. He'll be one hell of a looker. I'm assuming it's a boy. Can't imagine alpha male Shashi with a girl. What with his good looks? And she's drop-dead gorgeous too, isn't she? When I'd first met her in Singapore ten years ago, she was nothing like this, of course. She was just getting out of her failed relationship with that horrible Mohit Kanwar.'

I think my jaw drops open, and Tina notices as she takes a drag of her e-cigarette.

'Oh, you didn't know that, did you? Yes, she was seeing that horrible cricketer for years. He was such a womaniser. He kept trying to get his hands all over me when we'd met at a party. He married that actress Firdaus, no? We're family friends. Anyway, I was so glad when Laila met Shashi. He is so charming! Everything a woman wants. Sexy, smart, suave, charming. It was a good thing Shashi was able to get out of the whole alimony business with his first wife. I never did like her. Their marriage lasted three months but she was a nasty cookie, all right. Or so Laila tells me. Oh, you didn't know he was divorced?'

By now, my head is crammed with so much information, I feel like it's about to explode.

And then when I think I've had enough new information to digest, Tina Tej Mushran drops a bombshell.

'I wonder whether they'll give the baby Shashi's last name or Laila's.'

'The baby will get the father's surname, no?' I say.

'Yes, I suppose he will.' Tina inhales deeply. 'Though, of course, they're not married, so I'm assuming they'll have to have some legal adoption paperwork to sort out?'

Week 26

Your baby will now be moving around quite vigorously
and may even respond to loud noises

Mona

'Switch off the radio! It's too loud,' I complained to Rani.

'Still headache hai?' she asked me with great concern.

My head was splitting and I couldn't even have a painkiller. Rani was worried. She had ditched the veggies and made me chicken casserole to help me feel better. But nothing was working.

After Tina dropped the bomb on me, she whispered about how Shashi is not very sure about the baby at all. This pregnancy has been a strain on their relationship and they've even been seen arguing in public. He hadn't gone for a single scan with Laila. Yes, they've been travelling together, but she thinks Laila is painting a far rosier picture of their relationship than it really is. He isn't pleased about a baby at all.

He should've thought of that before unbuttoning her shirt in the living room with the windows wide open, I thought angrily.

I wanted Tina to leave right then. I thought my water was going to break, just picturing Laila going for all the scans on her own. And for going through this pregnancy all alone. No wonder she had been so friendly with my mothers and even with the whacko Shania. It's obviously because she has no family of her own, now that she's living in with a man who doesn't want to marry her. Poor, poor girl. Being a single mother can't be an easy task. How brave of her! And how unwelcoming I had been with her.

Right after Tina left, I bawled and bawled and bawled till Ramit got home and comforted me by saying it's best not to meddle in their private life.

But Laila is my friend.

Ramit

Mona really surprises me. I would have thought that hearing of an unmarried couple going through a pregnancy would have made her disapprove more of them. But instead of that, she is actually feeling sorry for Laila, and after she finally stopped crying, she sat down to work out a plan to help Laila with the pregnancy. She wants to go with Laila for the doctor visits and scans.

And then she bitched the shit out of Shashi.

I told her we should think it through and see how Laila wants to manage it. She's never told us about their relationship herself so it's best to give them space.

Then distracted her by planning a trip to Dehradun to see her folks before she's unable to travel. That made her cry even more. That she had a family she could go to and Laila had none.

Mona

Airports are such happy places and flying to Dehradun usually makes me happy, but this time I felt so low. Kept thinking about Laila. I'm sure she didn't want to tell us about their marital status because she's embarrassed to be having a baby out of wedlock.

And look at me! I'd been introducing her as Shashi's wife to so many people and she'd never bothered correcting me. She may have secretly wanted to be his wife but that man, that awful, horrible man, he doesn't want the baby or her. Well, that's not what Tina said exactly, but why won't he marry her now that she's pregnant!

Actually to think of it, no one ever introduced her as Shashi's wife. Laila never said it. Tina never did. I simply assumed they were a couple. A married couple.

And then I remember the shadow that crossed her face when I'd asked her where her folks were. Obviously her folks don't want to have anything to do with her. She's living in with a divorced man. She doesn't have any family.

And that made me burst into tears again.

Ramit

Been volleying calls from Mummy all morning. She is livid that I've taken time off for Dehradun and am not coming to Amritsar instead. She insists Mona will be better taken care of in Amritsar as there are lots more people to watch out for her and we as a family cumulatively have more experience with pregnant ladies.

Then she went on and on about how it should be a trip to Amritsar not Doon, if this is the last week Mona can fly safely without the doctor's permission.

Then she went on and on about how we should not be flying at all.

So I told her boarding was starting and switched off my phone, even though we had another hour to kill.

Mona

I'm a whole lot calmer by the time I get home. It's been a year since my last visit. Mom is thrilled and pottering around in what seems to be a cross between a patiali salwar and capris. I don't even know how to describe it. And Dad, he's meeting me for the first time since my pregnancy and he doesn't say anything about the bump.

'Ah Mona!' he says giving me a hug. 'Ramit, drink?'

Ramit

Being home lifted Mona's spirits. Some lady in a business suit walked in, carrying a briefcase, and it took me a minute to realize it was Shania. She's off her yogi phase and now claims to be studying fashion designing.

Mom brought out caramel cake and Mona looked pained. I recalled Laila asking for the recipe and realized Mona must have been thinking of it too.

Then when Mona's Mom asked how Laila was doing, Mona started sobbing. Made an excuse about pregnancy hormones. I think it's so sweet of Mona to not discuss Laila's situation with anyone. She wants to respect her privacy.

Her tears dried up when Mom announced that the buas were coming over for dinner. Which means Suhani bua with a suitcase full of tragic stories of doom and gloom.

Mona

I thought I had been successful in keeping my emotions under control this whole weekend – I tried not to think about

Laila, tried not to let Suhani bua's dreadful stories overwhelm me, tried not to get all weepy about Mom placing a cot in my room. And then, just as we were leaving for the airport, my dad came up to me and said that there was something he wanted me to see. He had spent the entire weekend discussing business and politics and God knows what all with Ramit, so I was surprised at him approaching *me* for a change!

He took me to his garage studio and presented me with this gorgeous painting of a mother and child, which simply glows off the canvas. I could feel the happiness on the mother's face as her eyes crinkled at the sight of the child. And the purity of the bond as the child gazed up at her.

'It's for you, Mona, my baby girl. It's to symbolize this journey, and I can't tell you how proud I am of what you've become. You'll make the most amazing mother. I love you, my baby.'

And just as he kissed the top of my head, I obviously burst into tears.

Laila doesn't have her father gifting her a painting at a time like this. Laila's child won't have a father either.

Ramit

I tell her people have kids outside their marriage all the time and maybe Tina was only exaggerating. Maybe Laila is indeed happy and maybe they just don't want to get married.

My wife thinks she's being all nice about the situation by not judging Laila's lifestyle but actually she is being quite invasive.

Week 27

Your baby's activities may make it harder for you
to sleep at night

Mona

Haven't been sleeping very well since the news about Laila. And the baby being so big and doing God knows what in there isn't helping things.

Anyway, finally decided on what to do and turned up at Laila's doorstep with a caramel cake early evening.

She was delighted and welcomed me in.

Now here was my plan. I would be honest with her and offer my help. I wanted her to know that we could be the family she doesn't have. She's not in this alone. That we would take her in if Shashi, the two-faced, evil @&#! wasn't being supportive. That I would go with her to the doctor. That I would be there.

But when I sat across from her and saw her cheerfully wolfing down the cake, I lost my nerve.

'So the next scan is due in another couple of weeks,' I said instead.

'It is? My doctor hasn't told me about it so I'm guessing it's further away for me.' She smiled at me angelically. She really is beautiful.

'Will Shashi be going with you?' I blurted stupidly.

She chewed on the cake for a bit and then pleasantly shook her head. 'No, I don't think so. He's typically quite busy with his work and anyway, doctor visits are just not his thing.' She snorted. 'And seriously, it's not like it's a surgery. It's just a scan. Don't know why they make a big deal about it.' I felt a bit sheepish about my excitement about the scan.

'Tina would go alone for her scans too,' Laila added. 'Especially during Sameer's time. I think by then Tej was so done with it.'

'I can come with you, if you like,' I offered.

She looked at me in surprise. 'Oh. That's very nice of you to offer. Thanks. But no, don't worry. I'll manage. I know Shimauli very well so it's no issue at all. Shimauli's my doctor. She always comes with me for the ultrasound.'

'Still. You shouldn't go for scans and doctor visits on your own.' I sounded as ancient as the mothers but I brushed that aside. This was for a good cause.

She smiled at me again, amused. 'It's all right, Mona. Don't worry about it. I'm used to it. In fact, I've lived on my own for fifteen years in Singapore. I've even been to the emergency room on my own multiple times. And it's so much easier here in India. I personally know the doctor and I can easily go on my own.'

So she basically admitted that she's alone. I blinked back tears and then decided to be blunt. 'Look. I know about you and Shashi. And I just want you to know...'

'About me and Shashi?'

'Yes, that you're ... not married. And I just want you to know that it must be very hard to be pregnant without being married.'

I noticed she'd stopped eating and was looking at me with a bit of a frown. She shrugged.

'Yeah, I wondered why you introduced me as his wife to your family. I always thought you were worried they would be, well, orthodox in their ways and judge us.'

What? Was she calling *my* family orthodox?

I cleared my throat. 'Um, no. I just thought because ... I mean you wear a wedding ring.'

Laila looked at her hand. 'Oh this? No, it's not a wedding ring. Just something I picked up from Tiffany's many years ago. Anyway, I know in India people do judge. But who cares about them?' She went back to her cake. 'I assumed you knew, most of our friends do. The domestic staff here talks the most about these things,' she snorted. 'They don't seem to get the whole living-in idea.' Was she comparing me to her domestic staff?

Then she smiled at me patronizingly. 'I know, it's a little odd in India to understand this, but it is okay, really. Shashi has had a bad experience with marriage, and well, it's all right by me too. I *so* cannot see myself being someone's wife!'

I couldn't believe it! Here I was, trying to be helpful about the situation she was in, and she was saying this was out of choice! She was taking pride in the fact that she was having a baby out of wedlock!

'Anyway, marriage is such an overrated institution. And ya, I got knocked up.' She laughed. 'But so be it. It's only a baby. You know, right, it's very common abroad.' She was making me sound like some desi ... some ancient ... orthodox ... some narrow-minded ... like Mrs Kapoor from the park! Like I was too uncool to understand their 'foreign' ways.

'Besides, I'm not a single mom, in that sense. Shashi and I are together. We don't really care what the "legal" status is. We're so much happier than so many married couples.' I swear she looked at me pointedly.

I wanted to snap back at her and tell her that her best friend Tina Tej Mushran has been bad-mouthing her in that case and been saying that Shashi is not really happy about the situation. She should be more careful about the friends she chooses, because which best friend goes around town revealing their friend's private lives to complete strangers? But I'd had enough. I made some excuse and took off.

And now I'm hopping mad.

Ramit

Mona called. She shouted at me for making her look like a fool in front of Laila. I told her to calm down, that Laila didn't mean anything and was perhaps just taken aback, to which Mona slammed the phone down on me after telling me that I, like her mother and her sister and like everyone else, am always taking Laila's side.

I'm so glad for cellphones. You can't slam them the way you would a landline.

Mona

Of course a baby must be born to two parents who are married to each other, rather than having to answer so many questions later in life! Especially when most children's parents are married.

I hope for the sake of the Sachdev-Haider child, that they move abroad with more 'like-minded' people than staying with 'narrow-minded' people like me.

I put my hand on my belly and had a word with my child. I hope he knows how lucky he is to have happily married parents.

Or she. It could be a she. With a big foot.

And then just as I was about to draw the curtains of the living room, I saw Laila puking out all the caramel cake I'd spent the morning baking for her.

I'm totally done with the bloody neighbours.

Week 28

Many women start getting heartburn and indigestion as
the baby grows

Mona

Bruce Lee is at it again. He's been kicking and jumping and bringing up all the acid my liver has ever produced right to my mouth. I nudged Ramit as he slept.

'Baby is jumping,' I informed him.

He turned the other way and promptly slept off again.

I nudged him harder and told him again. He turned towards me and slept off again.

Then I kicked him and he woke up.

I took his hand and placed it on my stomach.

Ramit

I had to let the crazy pregnant woman let me sleep so I made all sorts of appropriate noises about how the baby was moving and I could feel it and slept off with my hand on her stomach.

Mona

I've married the biggest liar in the world! The baby had totally stopped moving by then!

Ramit

So drowsy. Had to sit up most of the night rubbing Mona's back because she had acidity. I feel a bit sorry for her.

Made some joke about Aunty Acidity, that character whose jokes do the round on Whatsapp? Bad idea.

I don't know everything these hormones have done to my wife but they've definitely washed off any sense of humour she had.

Then she told me how acidity is a good thing. Apparently, the more the acidity, the more hair the baby's supposed to have.

So what, we're having a … *gorilla?* Thank god I didn't say that one out loud.

Mona

Feeling highly cheated now that I read up on the final trimester online. This is supposed to be the 'golden trimester', but here I am, suffering heartburn.

Ramit

Her tongue's turned quite acidic too. Laughed at that one too. To myself.

Mona

Good God! Ramit is simply rolling with laughter and refusing to tell me why. I debated whether to send him off to the couch or something, but then he finally fell asleep snickering.

ZARREEN KHAN 263

Now I'm trying to think of foods that don't give me acidity but I can't think of anything.

When I told Mom about it, she promptly told me to get a giant bottle of Gelusil. I told her to be a little more original. She says I'm as rude as Shania. Big insult that is!

Mummy, on the other hand, has sent me a massive bottle of smelly heeng to put in my food. If this is what they've been giving Mohini, I finally understand why she's been puking her guts out.

Ramit

Just don't get it. How can she be hungry with all this miserable heartburn?

Waiting for her to finish with her breakfast so that we can get to Dr Mehak's. I really have an urgent meeting but if I push this, Mona will crib about it non-stop.

Mona

So guess who surprised us! Ramit's Mummy. She turned up unannounced at our doorstep, saying she was so worried about my acidity she took the first flight in. Now she's pleased she can come with us to the doctor and discuss this acidity thing with her.

And guess who has a death wish. Ramit. He says he can now safely go for an urgent meeting and Mummy can take me to the doctor's.

So here we are now, being ushered into the doctor's room and all I can think about is if Dr Mehak is going to tell Mummy I'd asked her if it's safe to have sex during pregnancy. I'm so nervous. I could kill Ramit!

But Mummy's jaw has dropped open at the sight of Dr Mehak. She does look more like a college student in her red frames, red trinkets and her red-and-white dress.

When Dr Mehak asks me to come across to the examination table, Mummy stands up to accompany us.

'Oh, you can keep sitting, aunty,' Dr Mehak says politely. Mummy looks offended, perhaps at being called aunty or at being told what to do, don't know; but she shoots the doctor a stern look before taking a seat reluctantly. But it seems like Dr Mehak is immune to Mummy's crushing looks. Suddenly I respect my doctor a hundred times more.

Dr Mehak checks my abdomen and barks off some numbers about height of the uterus, etc. before putting on the Doppler. Every time I hear the baby's heartbeat, mine leaps about too.

Ramit

Mummy gave me an unsolicited character report of Dr Mehak when I got back from work.

'She's very young,' she told me as Mona slept on the couch. 'I went to Dr Bindra and she had thirty-four years' experience.'

'Dr Mehak is very well known and while she may look young, she is in her mid-forties.'

'That's too young,' she said, shaking her head. 'In doctory, you need to be well experienced.'

'In medicine.'

'Also in doctory.'

'There's no such thing as doctory, Mummy. It's medicine.'

Mummy looked at me like she was going to give me another earful about having the audacity to correct her, a school principal, but then sighed loudly. 'I can't believe it. I've forgotten my English. I have to find another job.'

I reached out and squeezed her hand sympathetically.

'Anyway,' she continued professionally, 'Dr Mehak wears too much jewellery. She has to take off those rings and necklaces when Mona goes into labour!'

'I'm sure she'll be careful not to hurt her, Mumma.'

'Hurt her? I meant it shouldn't fall in when she opens her up.'

'She's not opening her up. It's not an operation, you know. She just has to pull the kid out of the … You're just being paranoid!'

I thought Mummy would go on a tirade on how I almost said the V-word but she ended up ranting away about how I called her paranoid.

Mona

'This doctor of yours,' Mummy said, 'is a fashion queen.'

Ramit had warned me about this. She's trying to persuade us to change our doctor.

'You need to be better dressed around her,' she continued, patting my hand.

I am surrounded by the fashion police!

Be better dressed at this weight? Boy, I can't believe I've put on so much weight.

Ramit

I didn't think Mona was that big, but after dinner today, she got stuck between the table and chair. I kind of wanted to laugh but then pretended I hadn't noticed.

Mona

Phew! Thank God nobody saw that! How embarrassing for my ass to get stuck like that. Good thing Ramit had that coughing fit and was distracted.

Ramit

Mummy just told me that Mona should take her walks more seriously. Guess she saw that too.

Week 29

Braxton Hicks contractions start as a painless tightening that begin at the top of your uterine muscles and spread downwards

Mona

Started the morning with Suhani bua's weekly call of 'now you are in the most dangerous phase of your pregnancy, the seventh month'.

Dismissed it instantly.

And then…

Ramit

Rushed home. Got a panicked call from Mona. She was in the bathroom and said the contractions had started. And she's only seven months along. She was bawling.

I told Surjit Mona was unwell and got home to find Mona locked in the room. She didn't want Mummy to know and panic so we told her we had to meet a friend for lunch and smuggled out a bag of hastily packed clothes into the car.

Mona said she felt acute tightening of her stomach, and pain too.

'Back to front. Just like I've read about labour.'

I would have Googled but we had to get to Dr Mehak on time.

Mona

Injured. By the look Dr Mehak gave us. And by her assistant's snicker.

'Your contractions have started?' Dr Mehak asked, eyeing me sceptically. I nodded.

'At what interval?'

I looked at her blankly.

'I had one right here...' I said, pointing to the area on the top of my stomach. I assumed that's where my uterus must be now.

'And then?'

I blinked again.

'That was it.'

Apparently it was Braxton Hicks. False contractions. We were given a lowdown on how to identify actual labour.

I'm so embarrassed.

When we left, I told Ramit it was best to confess to Mummy. And so I got home and told her I had had contractions.

'It must've been Braxton Hicks,' Mummy said matter-of-factly.

'*You* know about Braxton Hicks?' Ramit asked doubtfully.

Mummy shot him one of her murderous looks. How dare he question her knowledge!

'You *don't* know about Braxton Hicks?' she bit back. 'It's in all the books I gave you. Have you not read them?'

Now he's sitting with his nose buried in the pile as if we have an exam to take.

Which is basically all right. It is his fault we panicked today. If he had taken this pregnancy seriously enough to read up on it earlier we could have avoided this situation.

Ramit

Thankfully the embarrassment of this morning has been forgotten as more exciting news has reached us this evening. Mohini is in labour.

Mummy is pacing up and down the room and regretting missing out on the chaos in Amritsar.

My mother has bitched about cousin Mohini ever since she announced her pregnancy but is now biting her nails and is constantly on the phone for updates.

Women!

Mona

Puking-her-guts-out Mohini has had a baby girl. They've named her Sohini. Very creative. Mohini ki Sohini. They'd thought of Mohan if it were a boy. Mohini ka Mohan. Now everyone is raving about what wonderful in-laws she has that have allowed her to rhyme the name with hers rather than her husband's. Her husband's name is Kulbhushan. Good luck rhyming anything with that!

By that logic, I should have Mona ka Shona. Or Mona ka Bona.

Ramit

Mummy gives me gory details of Mohini's labour and I beg her not to tell Mona.

Apparently Mohini even puked at the labour table. I've told Mom she needs to see a gastroenterologist at the earliest.

Week 30

By now you may begin to feel tired and uncomfortable more frequently

Mona

Gosh. I'm exhausted all the time! I felt like taking a nap after a shower but dreaded sending Mummy into a frenzy of concern. So I sat up and drank my juice obediently, trying to keep my eyes open as Mummy continued with her tales of the Deol family.

'Nayantara is just not getting along with Daisy,' she told me, knitting something grossly green. Like slime green. I hope to God it's not for my child. I placed a protective hand across my belly lest the unborn child saw it. Their eyes are open inside the uterus by now, you know. Oh God. There's a creature inside me with its eyes open. Ack!

'I think Daisy is too interfering,' Mummy went on. 'Do you know how much she pressured Nayantara to have a third child? She wants a boy. In this day and age! We would never meddle with your private lives. You and Ramit can decide to have one, two, three or no children at all. I mean, come on, you guys didn't want to have a family for four years and we didn't say anything. It's just so interfering of her! And Nishi, she's so desperately looking for a girl for Soham. I told her to calm down. He's only twenty-eight. We put no pressure on Ramit to get married. It was just because you both were in such a great hurry...'

I suddenly desperately wanted to escape that conversation and announced it was time for me to sort out the baby's clothes.

In any case, those pregnancy books say I should be nesting by now. Which I would have liked to interpret as building myself a nest and sleeping in it forever, but actually it means I should be sorting out the baby's wardrobe and nursery and all that jazz.

Ramit

Got home at seven sharp as per Mummy's rules. The house was empty. Thought maybe Mona and Mummy had gone shopping. Which meant I would get some more time to finish some pending work. Bonus time!

Then found a suitcase by the door. Panicked that Mummy and Mona had had a fight and Mummy was leaving. Prepared a hasty speech on how it was Mona's pregnancy hormones and Mummy should not take it seriously and decided to throw in some fake Google research too.

Then realized it looked like one of our suitcases. Opened it and found my clothes in it.

Spent the next half hour wondering what I had said to Mona that she would want to chuck me out. That's when Laila walked in.

'Oh! The hospital bags are packed already!'

Phew! That's what it was.

'Bit early, isn't it?' she asked.

Mona

Mummy and I made a list of all the missing things and went to the market to pick up diapers, formula and some other knick-knacks.

Received a call from Mom, who asked me my whereabouts and I told her I was shopping for the baby. She did the whole heartbroken number on me on how I could go shopping with my mother-in-law instead of her, but since I can't really be on my feet for very long, I abruptly cut her off and switched off my phone.

Got home to find a very leggy Laila in her tiniest shorts standing at the door and talking to Ramit. She flashed me a smile. I didn't really want to talk to her after the horrible chat the other day, so I forced one fake smile right back at her and pushed my way through the door.

'You look very nice!' I heard her say. I studied my brown pregnancy slacks and floral knee-length shirt and wondered what she was talking about. Then I heard Mummy reply, 'Oh thank you, darling. You look lovely yourself! Where did you get these shorts from? Are you allowed to wear them during your pregnancy?'

'Yes, Aunty, maternity,' she said, lifting her shirt, much to my horror, to show her the high waist band.

I saw Ramit's ears turning pink. He cleared his throat and mumbled something before walking off inside.

I wanted to follow him in and show him all my shopping, but Laila said, 'Hey, Mona, I came to ask if you're free for lunch tomorrow.'

Oh no. Not another one of her bashes. Or Tina's. Or worse, her baby shower. That Tina must have surely planned one.

'I … er…'

'There's this new place in Cyber Hub,' she said hastily, 'that has really nice brunches, so I thought maybe the two pregnant ladies could go make the most of their unlimited brunch offer.' I'm not sure of it, but I think the laugh that followed was strained and nervous.

'I don't know,' I said looking over at Mummy for help. She would say it's not good to eat out and how I was putting on too much weight or whatever, but it backfired.

'Excellent!' Mummy said instead. 'I told my cousin Vij that I'd come by tomorrow. So you both have lunch and then I can pick you up. Sounds good, Mona?'

Ramit

Mona is even more irritated than usual about Mummy being in town.

Told her to concentrate on the lovely brunch she can look forward to.

Wrong thing to say, apparently. Yes, have been sent to sleep in Mummy's room tonight.

Mona

I wore my maternity pants and my best maternity top and wore make-up and earrings, and, I swear, it looked like I was going on a date, but still, Laila Haider managed to outshine me in her yellow chiffon dress, her golden headband and her pregnancy glow. I probably looked like an old-fashioned shoe compared to her.

She met me very warmly at the restaurant and we got lots of amused looks by onlookers as we tried to hug each other despite our massive bellies. I squeezed into my chair and took 120 seconds to adjust my butt, while Laila glided in like she was right out of some finishing school.

We ordered from the buffet menu; thankfully Laila did not order wine, and I patted some loose hair into my bun as she stroked her silky brown hair.

'I'm so glad you could make it,' she said cheerfully.

'Why aren't you at work?' I asked her pointedly.

'Oh I just finished my last leg of travel so I thought I'd take a couple of days off,' she sing-songed. 'They don't allow you to travel after the twenty-eighth week on most domestic flights and Shashi is quite particular about us being careful, so I thought I'd finish it all off by the sixth month itself. Shimauli can easily issue me a letter that I'm fit to travel for another month or so, but Shashi, well no point arguing. Anyway, how are you keeping?'

I could have told her about the terrible nerve pain in my butt that makes me feel like I'm sitting on a hedgehog, but decide we were not 'close' enough.

'I'm doing totally fine,' I lied, taking a deep breath so that she wouldn't notice my breathlessness.

'That's great. I saw you've already got your bags ready. Exciting, isn't it, to be in the final leg?'

I don't know what she meant by exciting. I was scared and uncomfortable, but that was it. I nodded nonetheless.

'How is Shania? Will she be coming down anytime soon?'

I wanted to tell her that she would perhaps know that better than me since she is the sister Shania never had, as per my very own mother, but I made some vague comments and switched to even more random conversation about her job and Shania's fashion course. Our food arrived shortly and I was pleased to find an excuse to not talk.

It was only at dessert that she looked me in the eye and pursed her lips.

'I've been meaning to talk to you, Mona, about the other day.'

I felt so uncomfortable. She was now going to talk down at me for being nosy and interfering and old-fashioned. I debated whether to be on the offensive, or defensive. I'm no good with offensive so I tried to think of an excuse for my behaviour. Hormones. That's what Ramit keeps going on about.

'I'm really touched by your concern,' she said gently.

I looked at her for a hint of sarcasm but she looked, well, genuine.

'You know, a lot of people do assume Shashi and I are married and well, with the baby it's all the more uncomfortable admitting that we're not and that's why, I overreacted the other day.'

'Well, it wasn't my place…'

'Oh but it was,' she said squeezing my hands. I was definitely not expecting this.

'I feel so touched that you were concerned about me. You didn't judge me or my choices but actually came to lend me a helping hand. That hasn't happened with me in … years.'

She leaned back against her chair with a faraway look in her eyes. 'I have a lot of friends, Mona. Many of them I can count on; many of them are, well, just acquaintances. But I keep myself busy by having them around because, well, I don't have any family.' She looked at me with … envy?

'Gosh, I'm so jealous of you. You have your husband and in-laws and parents and sister … they all dote on you and they're always there for you and the baby. I have … well, Shashi.' Her eyes looked sad.

'I'm not used to people offering help. I've lived alone for so many years, dealt with so much shit, that I hate accepting help. I don't even like to acknowledge to myself that I *need* help. But you came by the other day and...'

'Where is your family?' Stupid thing to ask and be all nosy, but my tongue has a mind of its own.

'Well, I haven't seen my father since I was twelve. He's lived in the States, mostly. He moved after the divorce. My mother visits every now and then. But she's mostly in Australia now. I don't hear from her very often. The only family I have is my friends. Tina, to start with. Though it's only been a few years since I've known her, she really looks out for me. And there's Shashi...'

She bit her lip and I genuinely felt sorry for her. 'Well, I didn't think Shashi would take the baby thing so badly. I mean, it's not badly, really, but he's not very involved at all. He tried to reason with me on whether we should have this baby. After all, we were very clear about not getting married – he's had a bad experience. And he wondered if things would change and whether I'd want to get married now. But I'm okay. I am, really. As long as he, well, as long as he wants the child too. I know, of course, there are lots of upsides to being married, for the sake of your baby, but I don't want us to marry just *because* of a baby. And I'm really excited, you know. My very own family. For you, you have so much family. For me, my baby will be my own. For the first time. Mine.' She flashed me the warmest of smiles, cuddling her hands under her chin.

'And yes, I currently do feel a bit lonely. I mean, loneliness has never saddened me before and I like my space and, honestly, if my mum really does turn up, I wouldn't know what to do with her beyond an hour! But, you know, pregnancy hormones. They make you feel so happy and so sad all at the same time. So fulfilled yet so lonely. Sometimes I wonder whether I'll be able to do justice as a single parent. I mean, I know I'm not a single parent and that Shashi is there ... or will be there, once he sees how sweet the baby is.' A hint of doubt crossed her face but she shook her head and smiled at me.

'Anyway, I never had anyone offering me help. And so I wanted to thank you. Thank you for offering and thank you for not judging.'

I squirmed in my seat. I had judged her. I've judged her since the moment we'd met.

All I could think of now was how lonely Laila Sach ... Haider really must be to make these confessions to me, a total stranger. Almost a total stranger.

I reached out and squeezed her hand.

Ramit

I don't know what happened at lunch but the wife and the neighbour are suddenly best friends!

Crazy pregnant women!

Week 31

Rhinitis of pregnancy, or a widening of the nose
in the second and third trimester, is caused
by higher estrogen levels

Mona

Shania sent me a rude text about the picture I'd WhatsApped her from my lunch with Laila. 'What's going on with your nose? It looks like a trunk.'

'A tree trunk?'

'Like an elephant's trunk.'

I spent the entire morning checking myself out in the mirror. I always thought my nose was short and stubby but she's right. It does look rather odd now. Like it's growing.

Ramit

Mona has officially lost it. She wants to meet Dr Mehak to find out if it's okay for her nose to grow bigger.

Took me a minute to figure out whether she was talking about her own nose or the baby's.

Mona

Ramit was no help. Kept staring into his phone as usual.

So the next day, I asked Mummy if she could notice a difference in my nose to which she said, 'Yes, beta. You will have more mucus now, so you should keep it clean. Keep a tissue with you. Glad you noticed.'

Apparently I've been walking around like a snotty toddler and no one had bothered to tell me.

I should have got my nose pierced in college.

Ramit

Found Mona in front of the mirror when I got home, holding a ruler to her face.

Exited the room.

Mona

That insensitive twerp.

Spent the night mostly awake, wondering if I was actually going to become Pinocchio.

Heard Ramit sigh loudly and pull out his phone from under his pillow. He Googled nose expansion + pregnancy. Apparently it is a real thing. Some sort of nose growth during pregnancy. He first consoled me, then called me crazy and asked me to go to sleep.

Ramit

Mummy wanted to know whether Mona had been counting the baby's movement. Told her I didn't know. She snapped at me for not being an involved dad. I snapped at her and asked her whether Papa knew about my movements when she was expecting me. Then she snapped at me for snapping at her.

And in the midst of it Mona arrived with a red pen mark across her nose.

'If this mark moves in the next couple of days, I'll know it's not just my imagination and that my nose really is growing.'

'Are you not planning to wash your face for the next few days then?' I asked her.

Mona looked like she was about to cry – she had obviously not thought this through. Mummy hugged her and then snapped at me for being rude to her pregnant daughter-in-law and said Mona would make a gorgeous mother.

So that's basically what I should have said rather than bringing up her pregnancy brain.

Mona

Ramit looked all sheepish when he came into bed, apologising for not complimenting me enough, but the baby had started kicking again, so I put his hand on my stomach and he grinned at me.

It's magical!

Ramit

Still can't feel a damn thing.

Week 32

There will be another scan to check the position
of the baby

Mona

The final scan before the delivery is scheduled for this morning. We first went to see Dr Ram Rathore and then headed out to meet Dr Mehak in the afternoon. She's unavailable for the rest of the week as she has a wedding to attend in Thailand.

What if I go into labour! I started palpitating.

Ramit

Change of guards happened this morning. Mummy left for Amritsar. Mom arrived from Dehradun. Their paths did not cross. All is good in the world.

Mona

Shocked beyond words to see Mom in a grey pant suit. Shocked!

Everything matched. The cream shirt, the grey pants, the cream loafers, the cream hand bag.

Apparently Shania has completed two courses on fashion designing online and is experimenting on Mom .

I have never been more delighted.

Ramit

If any of the earlier ultrasounds had seemed miraculous, they paled in comparison to this one.

Dr Ram Rathore switched to the 3D mode today. And today, that alien-looking child of ours with Skeletor-like sockets and bony structure suddenly had flesh everywhere. He had chubby cheeks and Mona's tiny nose, and he was sucking his little thumb.

I could not believe the clarity with which technology now allowed us to see inside the body.

The only glitch was the, um, boy parts – well, they *could* have been the umbilical cord, after all. Because everything was all loose and floaty and long today.

So maybe, there still is a chance that it's a girl. With a large foot.

Mona

After a magical morning and Dr Mehak's positive comments on my progress and me feeling like a star pupil, she asked us whether we'd booked the hospital she delivers at.

So Ramit being all dutiful husband-like, spoke up in her clinic for the first time and asked her the name of the hospital she practises in.

Ramit

WHAT!

Mona

Ramit's jaw dropped to his knees. How embarrassing!

Ramit

I cannot believe I heard that! I cannot believe it. She can't be serious. I glanced at Mona who gave me a tight smile. She knew. Obviously she knew. What kind of dimwit doesn't bother asking which hospital they'll be having the baby at? But she can't be serious about that name!

Finally, I cleared my throat.

'I'm sorry, Dr Mehak, I didn't get the name of the hospital,' I managed to say.

She looked up at me with a deadpan expression and said, matter-of-factly, 'Tits and Tots.'

Mona

Ramit threw a fit when we got home and said there was no way we were having our baby at a hospital called 'Tits and Tots'. It sounds obscene, he said.

I have to admit that I had never bothered asking what the full name of T&T Hospital was, and this I was not prepared for, but Ramit is overreacting, really. There's no need to be pacing up and down like that.

Ramit

How can we even consider this hospital! Why are we even going to this doctor? What will we tell our child all his life?

How can we embarrass him like this? How will we tell people where to come visit us?

Mona

So I told Ramit it was all the better because I *don't* want people visiting us at the hospital, only close family. To which he had the gall to say that the bheed *is* family and they will all want to be there.

That's what I heard.

That they will all want to be there.

They. Will. All. Want. To. Be. There.

All.

ALL!

Ramit

Crazy pregnant woman is now huffing and puffing about how I could even dare to consider calling the entire bheed over. She tells me I'm crazy about going crazy over just the hospital name when I'm clearly the one doing the craziest thing of all.

I decide to storm out of the room and sulk in the drawing room and start looking for other doctors and hospitals we could go to. I know changing the doctor at such a crucial stage is terrible but Tits and Tots? No!

Mona

ALL!

He thinks we're calling ALL the relatives to view my labour.

He wants us to split up right before our first child comes into this world. That's what he wants.

Ramit

Googled all the maternity hospitals and doctors in the city. There's some La Enfante or something. Laila's going there. Decided we should just get Mona to switch to that too.

And there's some T&T which is very well known … Oh.

Mona

Ramit is calmer, now that he's found out that the hospital is actually called Teats and Tots and while honestly, it still sounds like Tits and Tots to me, I'm not walking down that path. I don't want to change my doctor at this stage. Not after fighting with the mothers over it and winning! He is now Googling the meaning of teat.

I find Mom tutting away at the 3D scan, turning it left to right, up to down.

'It just looks like a giant orange mess. What face are you even talking about?'

So when I send the image to Mummy and Shania and Laila, I include comments and arrows to title the parts of the face.

The younger women coo at it. The mothers just don't get it.

'Can't wait for my scan!' Laila texts me.

I know I'm being competitive, but can't help feeling smug about being four weeks ahead of her. Or three. Or whatever.

Then just before we get into bed, I have an emotional meltdown and make Ramit promise that none of his relatives will turn up to see me till I am back home, wearing nice clothes and till my hair has been blow-dried.

Week 33

Start making preparations for the new baby

Ramit

Top secret agenda underway. At 10 a.m. on Saturday I announced that we needed to finish off the baby shopping. Mona, who looked exhausted after being awake for thirty whole minutes today, tried to postpone it. I was insistent. Mona's Mom kept looking at the watch.

After plenty of complaints and drama, we left the house at noon.

Mona

My mother is the queen of emotional drama. When I had gone shopping with Ramit's mother she had created such a hue and cry about not being included in the experience and preparation. But today when we finally decided to go shopping, she wanted to stay home and relax.

'Enjoy your time alone!' she said, cheerfully bidding us good-bye.

'But you wanted to be a part of this,' I hissed at her.

'Oh well, next time,' she said dismissively.

'There won't be a next time! I only have three items left on the list.'

'Four, actually. Here, Ramit, beta. Mona's Dad has sent this money for her. Buy her a lovely maternity dress!'

'I'm thirty-three weeks pregnant! Why will I need a maternity dress now!'

'Doesn't hurt to be well dressed,' she reasoned.

'This is ridiculous! I'm not taking this money!' I complained.

'Take it!'

'No!'

'Take it!'

'No!'

'Mona!'

'Mom!'

'It's from your father!'

'I'll take it but not for me. I'll buy something for the baby!'

Then randomly Ramit snatched the money from us and walked off to the car.

Then, later, something got into him. He wanted us to have lunch out. I told him I had too much acidity and didn't want to eat at all but he insisted we grab a salad. A salad! I turned my nose up at it and ate a loaded cheese taco instead.

Then we walked at snail's pace through the stores. Ramit even stopped at a book store. He who does not read anything beyond his phone! And anyway, did he not realize how terribly uncomfortable I was?

And then he took me to this uber-expensive store and asked me to buy a dress. I refused but he insisted. And then when I finally dressed in a lovely red, chiffon knee-length kind of dream, he said we were buying it. Without looking at the price tag. And what's worse, he insisted I keep it on. He created such a scene by snatching up my maternity slacks and shirt and shoving them into the bag that I had to leave the store in embarrassment. Now I'm walking around the mall dressed like I'm off to prom night.

By 4 p.m., I wanted to kill him.

Ramit

Shania sent me a text saying they were ready. So I drove Mona home. She glared at me the whole way.

The amount of excitement and coordination we went through … and this is the mood I've put her in!

Mona

I HAVE THE MOST AMAZING FAMILY AND FRIENDS!

They threw me the most gorgeous baby shower in the world!

Mummy flew down from Amritsar, Shania apparently had been here all night without my knowing it. Laila and Tina helped with the planning, and my friends, who I haven't seen in so long, were all there! Along with a bunch of strangers who claimed to be Shania's friends but whatever. And even the bheed cousins were full of fun.

They made me wear a crown that said mom-to-be and we played games with bibs and diapers and everyone clicked pictures with me and they teased Ramit, whose rabbit ears stayed red all evening. Then I cut this gorgeous baby cake (though it was a bit weird to bite into a baby's bum) but it was deliciously chocolatey inside.

Tina Tej Mushran raved about the cake and the baker she'd hired to do this for us. Mom was back to her old fashion sense, dressed in a yellow and black sari – she looked like a local taxi. Turns out she had fought with Shania right before the party and didn't want her fashion advice. And Mummy was too busy with the Deol women to argue with my Mom. So there was basically a lot of peace and fun and laughter and it seemed like even Laila was enjoying herself with the crazy Deols.

And Ramit, oh Ramit was sooooo funny!

Ramit

I was asked, if the baby's hungry and Mona isn't at home, what would you feed the baby?

Apparently, the right answer is Cerelac. Not Nerolac.

Cerelac is cereal. Nerolac is paint.

Mona

Flooded with gorgeous baby clothes. I held some up against my face and nuzzled them.

'You know this new born baby smell everyone keeps talking about?' Shania whispered to me. 'I personally think they stink. I went to see Rustam's baby last week. Argh! Clearly you mothers lose all sense of smell after the delivery.'

She was browsing Facebook. 'Look at this baby. Now look at this one. They look the same, no? Bloody can't tell babies apart. Even your cousin Mohini's baby ... Wait, why is she on my friends' list? Unfriend!'

Week 34

Research shows that reading or talking to the baby helps
it develop its language skills

Mona

Walked across to Laila's house and it was filled with music. Laila was sitting on her couch, working on some presentation and listening to Western classical music. Beethoven or something. Maybe. I don't know.

She was pleased to see me.

'How've you been?'

'Waddling away,' I confessed. 'You haven't gone to work today, I noticed. Feeling all right?'

'I have to meet Dr Shimauli at noon so I thought I'd work from home before that.'

'What's with the music?'

'Oh, you're supposed to listen to lots of classical music when you're pregnant. It raises an intelligent child.'

And all this while I've been listening to remixes by DJ Suketu. My poor baby!

'I've also started reading books aloud,' Laila told me, pointing to a book on the table.

'Pride and Prejudice?'

'My favourite! Best thing to read to a baby, no? So beautifully written.'

And the last book I read was the *Cosmo*! Twenty-one ways to brighten your skin. What kind of frivolous mindless baby was I going to bring into this world!

'Sure, sure. Anyway, thank you so much for organizing the baby shower last week.'

'Oh no. It was all Shania's doing. She is thrilled about becoming an aunt,' Laila said, smiling.

Shania? The one who said kids stink and all of them look alike?

'Yes, I guess,' I muttered. 'Anyway, when does your maternity leave start?'

'I guess I'll try and work till the end. That way I'll get three months off after the baby. Tina's jappa will be here for six months, anyway.'

'Jappa?'

'Oh, haven't you heard of them? They're these baby nannies who do everything for your baby. Tina had one for all her babies.'

I made a mental note to ask Ramit.

'How does one get a jappa?'

'Hmmm. I'll ask Tina. They're not very cheap, let me warn you. 20K odd.'

I made a mental note to *con* Ramit.

Ramit

I'm sorry Mona, but I'm not hiring some jappa-wappa for 20 thousand a month! Mummy can come stay with us instead.

End of story!

Mona

Does he think his Mummy is some sort of a maid?

And then it struck me. This pregnancy is not the end of people staying with us. We'll be hosting the mothers for years to come!

Ramit

And now we're listening to Beethoven. Why? Because Laila has told Mona that listening to classical music helps develop the baby's intellect.

This is a Deol baby. Does Mona not understand that not much can be done about their intelligence? In fact, I'm sure that a live concert by Beethoven also would not do much about our baby's intelligence.

Mona

Of course I know it's a Deol baby. It therefore needs all the help it can get!

Uff!

Decided to read to the baby. Can't find a single decent book in this house. Started reading the leather-bound *National Geographic* series that sits in our drawing room as a show piece. Fell asleep on page two.

Ramit

Laila was over in the evening when I got back. She showed me a 3D scan of her baby. Very sharp features, like the parents.

Then she said to Mona, 'I don't know if you feel like it, but every time I walk into the maternity clinic I feel so … animal-like! You suddenly feel like a pregnant dog or a pregnant cow and generally, it's nature's doing at large. It's the most primal instinct, isn't it, to make a baby? To have sex?'

Mona

Ramit's ears flaming again as he excused himself. Can't handle any sort of sex talk! I must admit I blushed too and quickly changed the subject.

But after some time, Laila's excitement sobered down and she got a bit misty-eyed. She said she has to start shopping and wondered if I would like to help her? I'm assuming Shashi isn't being very helpful.

I really wonder how much longer they'll be able to hold on to this relationship.

I got misty-eyed myself.

Ramit

I left them talking about sex fifteen minutes ago and now they're crying.

I can never imagine men crying while discussing sex. Women are impossible to understand.

Week 35

Get a pedicure. It may be hard for you to reach that hard
skin on your feet now that you bump is in the way

Ramit

Mona is mighty excited that Laila and she are off to an afternoon of indulgence and beautification. She asked me about a million times whether I'm okay being home alone on a Saturday but I've told her to just go. Besides, I'm not alone. Rani is here, making me a feast. And since next week Shania will be here, this peace I deserve.

Mona

So here we are, getting lovely head massages, manicures and blow-dries when Laila calls the girl and orders two pedicures.

'Pedicure? During pregnancy?' I ask.

'Of course. Why not?'

Here's the thing. One of the initial few instructions Mom had barked down upon me had been 'no pedicures during pregnancy'. Apparently some pressure points on your feet send you into labour.

I was about to tell Laila just as much when Tina Tej walked in and planted herself on the chair next to mine.

'One pedicure and head massage,' she ordered, immediately sinking her feet into the tub.

Now I didn't want to sound like a paranoid soul. Especially since I'm anyway thirty-five weeks pregnant and the baby is fully formed and it's safe to go into labour. But what if Laila …

Ramit

Mona's Mom called me to say Mona wasn't answering her phone. I told her she was at the parlour. She asked me what for. As if I'm supposed to know the details!

I dialled Mona and asked her to call Mom back.

'I can't!' she said.

'Why?'

'Because I'm getting a pedicure!'

'But that's for the feet, right? Why are your hands not free to make a call?'

'Because if Mom finds out I'm getting a pedicure she will freak out.'

'Because she doesn't like clean feet?'

'Because she believes pedicures induce labour.'

'And is it inducing labour?'

She didn't respond, so I called but the line got disconnected. And then her phone went off.

I wasted the full afternoon panicking.

Anyway, she got back finally and there were no signs of labour.

Then she told me how relaxing it was and how Laila kept making these orgasmic sounds and Mona kept wondering if Laila was confusing labour for orgasms. And then Mona laughed and laughed about how my ears turned red at the O-word.

Week 36

Don't leave any crucial preparations for the baby's arrival for the last minute

Mona

I never, ever thought I would admire Shania's guts.

She turned up this morning and announced she was off for a belly dancing class.

'And how does that suit your fashion designer career journey?'

'Well, it doesn't. But it does broaden my horizons. It's with the ashram gang, anyway. They believe belly dancing is a great stress reliever. Om Shanti Shanti Peace Peace Shanti!'

Oh no! I'd never known a phase to return, but now ... she started giggling.

'Don't worry. I'm off saris and ashrams. Besides, Dad kind of, well, he was a little put-off by my sari style.'

Dad! He never says anything. She must've really offended him!

'What did he say?'

'He said I should audition for Baywatch. How can a sari be offensive, di?'

I didn't want to argue with her. 'So then *why* are you going for this belly dancing ashram thing again?'

'There was this really cute guy at the ashram, he's going to be there.'

Had to be a guy.

Ramit

A guy who's doing belly dancing?

I wanted to say something, but decided it was best if I stayed hooked on to my phone.

Mona

My feet really hurt a lot nowadays. So when Shania got home, I was sitting with my feet up. I told her a massage would help. And she obliged! Maybe she is growing up!

Then I wondered aloud who Laila would be turning to when her feet hurt.

'To her husband, of course,' Shania said scornfully. 'This is the husband's job, not a poor, tired-from-belly-dancing sister's.'

'Well, screw your belly dancing. If you think I'm going to get angry and pull my feet away at your rudeness, you're wrong. I mean, I am angry, but I'm not pulling my feet away.' I let her continue the massage and though she dug her bony knuckles deeper in the attempt to get fired, it was better than nothing, so I lay back and closed my eyes, bearing the pain with the pleasure.

'Anyway, he's not her husband, you know,' I added casually.

'Who?'

'Shashi. They're not married.'

Shania stopped and stared at me. 'What?'

'He's not her husband. He's her boyfriend. And he's been giving her a hard time with this whole baby thing. Apparently doesn't acknowledge it at all and she's really going through this whole thing on her own.'

Shania just sat in shock and stared at me. I cracked one eye open and told her to continue. Her hands became gentler as she prodded me for more information, which I gave her. Then she looked away thoughtfully and I wondered if she'd finally seen the sense in not having a baby without being married first. It's a lot of hard work.

But then, oh my God, I wondered if she was thinking that she now had a chance with Shashi since he wasn't married. I mean, the guy looks like Milind Soman and he's single! Kind of.

Ramit

So the sister-in-law, being what she is, stormed into the Sachdev household and created pandemonium. I could not believe it and would not have even known of it if Mona hadn't asked me to draw the curtains downstairs before retiring to bed. So I went paddling down and looked out of the window to find Shania standing in our neighbour's living room, waving her arms around in giant circles and being quite animated. Shashi Sachdev was standing with his arms crossed and Laila was sitting forlornly on a chair. I couldn't understand at all, but decided to leave it for the next morning. Why let Mona's crazy sister ruin our sleep!

I only broached the topic this morning at the breakfast table and asked Shania what she'd been upto at the Sachdev household. She told me she'd gone for a chat.

'First of all,' she added, 'it's not the Sachdev household. It's Laila and Shashi's house. They've bought it together. And Laila is not a Sachdev. Not yet, anyway.'

Mona raised an eyebrow at her.

'Secondly, they needed my help. I know they didn't ask me for it but I've liked Laila since day one and we've been in touch, so I couldn't just sit here and pity her situation after what di told me last night. Besides, I'm a certified counsellor. You guys know that, right?'

'You're a what?' Mona asked in horror.

'And what did you tell them?' I asked.

'I just helped them sort out their differences.'

'You did what?' Mona asked again.

'And are their differences sorted?' I asked sarcastically.

Shania munched her cereal thoughtfully. 'In my experience, I'll give it a week.'

Mona

I no longer know how to face Laila. I was finally beginning to like her and she was beginning to like me and now she'll think I'm some sort of loudmouth, discussing her private life with my immature sister who thinks she's some sort of certified counsellor. I think the only person who really needs counselling is Shania. And maybe Mom, because her mismatched dressing sense is really an outcome of her mismatched mind. And maybe Dad, because he just lives inside his canvas and paints and hasn't really been really present in the real world for years. And maybe Ramit, because he doesn't look up from his phone. And Mummy because she's just so bossy.

And maybe, me. Because I don't know why I'm so mean to everyone and why I can't use my brains on my business idea instead of wasting it all the time on judging people.

Ramit

Laila turned up looking pale. Asked to see Shania and they're now huddled in Shania's room.

Mona was moaning about how she wasn't included and how Laila must be mad at her.

Then Shania walked out and patted Mona's arm and said Mona can't be included in this because she's pregnant and she shouldn't stress herself out and Shania has the situation under control.

Mona

Situation under control! She hasn't had anything under control ever!

I called Mom but she disconnected. Then I called her again.

This time she spoke in hushed tones. 'Suhani is here. With yet another morbid story. I'll call you later, okay?'

Week 37

Your belly may look as though it's started to slide down

Mona

Everyone now has an opinion on when I am going to go into labour.

To start with, my doctor.

I went for a visit and she asked me to come weekly now.

'Oh Mona, any time now. Perhaps it'll be this week.'

Mom has been panicking because she's invited the buas for tea on Saturday and won't be able to make it if I go into labour. My very own mother is planning to miss my labour, something she has dreamed of for the last four years, because of her tea party? I told her as much but it fell on deaf ears.

On the other hand, Mummy told Bade Papa and he spoke to the airport guys and apparently now she's allowed to board a plane to Delhi within a half hour notice.

In fact, she was boasting that now every time a flight leaves for Delhi, someone from the airport calls her before they close boarding. Mummy's exaggeration is really becoming too Amritsari for its own good.

Also, Shania showed me *her* hospital bag.

'Why?' I ask her.

323

'Arrey! You think jeejs is going to stay with you overnight?
No. The mothers will insist he get some rest and they will
fight like Superman and Batman to stay with you. And guess
who you'll be wishing you had asked earlier. Me. So I might
as well be prepared.'

The probability of that situation did seem very high. So I
decided to pay special attention to her packing. I had to reject
three outfits on account of being too bold.

'I'm a designer now, di. This is fashion. You can't stop me.'

'This really looks like a slutty nurse outfit.' I said, and then
worried that she had chosen it precisely for that reason.

Ramit

On Sunday, Mona and I decided to get some fresh air and
went for a stroll in the park. Suhani bua had told Mona some
horror story about a neighbour going into labour during her
evening walk. Since Mona really wants the baby out now , it
seemed like a good option to try. Only, she waddled more
than walked. I wanted to call her Donald Duck but then good
sense prevailed.

Some woman in ankle-high sports shoes and salwar suit
with her dupatta knotted on the side immediately dashed
across to us.

'Aap Mr Deol?' she asked me excitedly.

I looked over at Mona, who introduced the lady as Mrs
Kapoor.

She immediately scanned Mona's belly.

'It's still very much high. No chance of labour right now.'

Seems like everyone's a doctor now.

Mona

Ramit's Mummy called me, sounding highly irritable. Something about 'these people' and pregnancies. I guessed she was talking about the Deols. Look, to be fair, Mummy is fairly reasonable and intelligent and doesn't deserve to be labelled a Deol. Much like me. And now she's stuck with them all the time. No wonder she's happy to drop everything and rush to Delhi to be with us.

But then again, I'm not taking that bait and inviting her over just yet. I need my peace. Even though Shania is really no peace at all. Yesterday she had a serious conversation with me about breast implants. First I thought she was suggesting it for me. Me. I'm currently size 38C. But apparently she's considering it for herself.

Anyway, Mummy sounded highly distressed, so I asked her what was wrong.

'It's about Mohini.'

Oh no! Her puking. Ramit had suggested taking her to the gastroenterologist. And now ...

'She's pregnant again.'

'No, Mummy, you must be mistaken. She just had her baby.'

'Her baby is two-months old.'

I didn't know people could get pregnant that quickly. Clearly Mohini didn't know either.

'Why doesn't she stay at her in-laws? She's always here, puking away,' Mummy complained.

Maybe it's because she's always puking away ...

Week 38

Your pregnancy is now full term

Ramit

Laila and Shashi came over today. We were all gathered in the living room – Mona, Shania and I.

'We wanted to speak with you guys.'

I wanted to run. Shania had meddled in their private lives and they were here to tell us off. I wanted to say or do something to show them that I wasn't complicit in the actions of wife or my sister-in-law.

'Sure, come on in,' Mona invited them, smiling widely. I looked over at her but she seemed all innocent.

'We can't stay very long. We have a lot of things to do.' Shashi said.

They never turn down an invitation, so I knew for sure that this must have been serious. Gosh, Shania is more trouble than all Deols put together. And there are a lot of Deols to put together …

'I can't thank you enough, Shania, for having this chat with us,' Laila said. 'You really helped us move forward in our relationship, and helped us open up to each other about what we want from our lives. And we've decided that since we're already bound by this beautiful life to come, we should bind ourselves in something else as well. So, we're getting married!'

Oh, getting married. Phew.

After that there was a whole lot of drama – Shania and Mona screaming and hugging Laila and Shania saying she knew it, she knew it and then the three women were squeezing each other's hands and talking non-stop. Shashi and I looked on. I figured I should say something to him too, so I smiled and said, 'what's up', to which he looked a little confused and shrugged. Clearly, 'what's up' was not the right response.

Mona

Basically all it needed was a little bit of mediation and counselling, and Shania helped them. She counselled Laila through her fear of losing someone again, like she had her cricketer boyfriend. She counselled Shashi about his broken marriage. Then she helped them express themselves with each other honestly and also gave them a little bit of emotional drama too, I think. Honestly, I can't believe this is my little sister of the ashrams and slinky saris. Wow.

And turns out, Shashi comes from a happy home and knows the importance of it. Laila comes from a broken home and yearns for her child to have a happy childhood. So all that was stopping them from making their relationship official was the fear inside them.

Apparently, Shania's counselling didn't tell them to get married or anything. She simply helped them 'arrive' at this resolution themselves.

'That's what counsellors do,' Shania told me. 'They *guide* you rather than *tell* you. Haven't you seen *Dear Zindagi*?'

Oh God! Was my sister claiming to be a counsellor because she'd seen one Bollywood movie on the subject?

But basically a lot of credit was given to Shania and how mature she was and I did feel a teeny weeny bit bad because I thought I had been helpful too by ... I'm not sure how, but I'm sure I'd been helpful.

Yes, I sometimes get competitive even with my baby sister.

Then they surprised me by asking me to be a witness at their registration. They're obviously having a court wedding. Me! Not Shania. Me!

Okay, it's a little unfair, because she's the one who helped them through this but ... wow! I've never been a witness in a court wedding before.

And it's next week!

Ramit

I don't want to burst Mona's happy bubble about being asked to be the witness instead of Shania, but it's clearly because Mona's the one with the Delhi residence proof, not Shania, and that's required for a court marriage. But she's so excited about it that now she's sitting with a paper and pen practising her signature.

Mona

Shania was sulking at not being asked to be the witness, but then they gave her this lovely semi-precious bracelet as a thank you gift so she was all right after all.

They will be having a civil wedding this Saturday at their house.

I had to tell Laila to keep someone else as back-up lest I go into labour; I'm 38 weeks now, you know. I could go into labour any second!

Dr Mehak did an internal check this week – painful and how – and said she's sure I'll be in this week itself.

But I don't want to let Laila down.

Ramit

The Saturday of the wedding, I had an urgent meeting come up. Mona was livid I had to go, but I promised I'd be back on time. Rushed back an hour late. Mona and Shania had left for the wedding next-door. It was noon, so assumed the signing was over. Shit. I'd missed Mona's moment of glory.

Took a quick shower and found Mona hadn't taken out my clothes for the wedding. Fine, it's a little chauvinistic of me to expect her to get my clothes ready, but I had a meeting this morning and … anyway, spent an hour trying to locate my sherwani. Finally found it in the guest room cupboard, thankfully dry cleaned and ironed. Quickly got ready and headed to the neighbours.

Mona

Gorgeous wedding! Lots of pink roses and a canopy of white lillies, where they took their vows. Shania, Tina and I had spent all of last week making preparations for the wedding.

I posed for a picture with Laila with our bumps. Felt more like a baby shower picture but whatever.

I was a bit sad that Ramit missed out on seeing me sign as a witness. My signature looked really classy. And I thought I looked really classy too. I was in my red dress from my baby shower, Shania was in a lovely green dress and Laila was in the most exquisite pink-and-white satin. All the men were in really smart tuxedos. Except …

Ramit

So it was more of a Western-style wedding. Right.

My sherwani was a bit of a fashion misfire.

Mona

Went back to my house to pee. Laila's loo was occupied. Just as I was coming out, I spotted Mrs Kapoor hiding behind one of the bushes, looking into Laila's house.

'Well, hello,' I said to her. She almost jumped out of her skin. Ha!

'Is there another party at that Laila's house?' she asked me.

'Yes, there is.'

'Big party. I've never seen them have such a big party.'

'Saheb-memsahib ki shaadi hai,' I heard Lakshmibai comment from behind me.

Mrs Kapoor looked indignant. She instantly dismissed Lakshmi. 'I was just asking like that only. Must be a milestone anniversary.'

'Not anniversary. Shaadi hai!' Lakshmi said loudly, as if Mrs Kapoor was deaf.

Mrs Kapoor looked at her in horror and then turned to me. 'But she's pregnant, na?'

'They're getting married now and yes she's pregnant and I'm really very happy for them,' I told her firmly.

'This is just too much modern for me,' she shook her head and walked off.

I hurried back inside and bumped into a mopey looking Tina Tej Mushran.

'This one's going to be hard to beat.'

'Sorry?'

'I've been planning her baby shower, you know. But after this party, I'm not sure how I'm going to throw something more grand.'

This was her wedding. It was supposed to be grand. And all this woman could think about was how to beat it! So competitive.

Ramit

I stood around like an oddball in my dark grey sherwani while all the other men walked around in their suits. I looked like the bandwala!

So I basically hung around the waiters and then walked off to the backyard and guess who I saw there. Shania. Exercising her mouth on a very handsome stranger. Mona came out just then too.

She pulled Shania aside and gave her a lecture on how she should have some dignity and shame and not do such things in public places with strangers. Shania rolled her eyes at Mona and called her old-fashioned. She said Ved was Shashi's nephew and while he was a wee bit younger than her, they had clicked. Called Mona a pregnant, hormonal aunty and swished off.

Mona

Just as we were retiring for the night I felt a stab of envy. What a beautiful wedding. White and pink. My own wedding had been red and gold, and very circus-like, with the mothers arguing throughout.

Then I felt another stab of envy as I recalled Laila squeezing my arm this afternoon.

'Shit!' she'd said with a laugh. 'I never thought I'd wear a size ten for my wedding!'

Size ten! I couldn't even wear a size ten *before* my pregnancy!

And then just before I closed my eyes, I wondered, would Laila have a wedding night?

Week 39

Every small twinge has you on high alert

Mona

This morning, I opened the door to find Leela, Laila's maid, standing at the door.

'Didi, Madam ...' she said, breaking into a sob.

All sorts of things came rushing to my mind.

He'd killed her! He'd killed her on their wedding night! He didn't really want to marry her. He never had. She had emotionally blackmailed him. And now he'd killed her.

'Madam ... floor pe ...'

I rushed to their place and found Laila on their sofa, twisting in pain, a pool of water around her feet. I froze in shock.

'What do we do? What do we do?' Leela kept rambling, wringing her hands.

'Mona,' Laila managed to say, grasping my hand. 'I think I'm in labour. I mean,' she managed to laugh, 'I am definitely in labour. And Shashi is in court.'

Oh my God! His wife was in labour and he'd gone to file for divorce! Then I remembered he was a lawyer.

'I've sent word to him but ... arrrrrrgggg ... phoo phoo phoo ...'

I felt like my own water would break in panic.

'So he didn't hurt you?'

'Who didn't hurt me?'

'Shashi?'

'What? No, I'm in … aaaaa … contraction … phoo phoo phoo.'

I quickly gathered my wits.

'Call my husband,' I told Leela.

I stroked Laila's hands. 'Don't worry. Ramit will drive us to the hospital immediately. He's still home. Where are your papers?'

'They're right here in the top drawer. You'll need to call my doctor Shimauli and tell her I'm coming in. I haven't even done that yet. I could only think of Shashi. I thought …' Another contraction and she broke into a hysterical scream. 'I thought I could hold on till Shashi got back but this … argh! Phoo phoo phoo … Yes, don't think I can. Oh Mona, it's so bad, so bad!'

I felt a sympathy contraction myself. I didn't want to know how bad it was.

'I had a few … in the morning when Shashi was … leaving. But after that I was just sitting here and my water broke!' She yelped out again. Okay, clearly the contractions were coming faster now.

I called Dr Shimauli and told her Laila was coming in.

Ramit came rushing in, looking panicked, and put a hand on my stomach.

'I'm not in labour. She is! Hurry up! Get the car out.'

As Ramit went dashing out, I heard Laila snicker between her screams.

'Shit, Mona. I thought it only happened in the movies …
that you have sex … and it induces labour.'

Ramit

They had sex on their wedding night. Which is fine. But she
was pregnant. Mona hasn't let me near her in nine months. I
glanced at her and she looked back pointedly.

No point discussing that, then.

We rushed in and were given curious glances by the
hospital staff.

'Umm, which one of the ladies is in labour?'

Fair question, since Mona was sweating and huffing and
puffing and generally far more panicked than the woman in
labour.

They wheeled Laila in and Mona went in with her. I was
glad to see Shashi rushing in five minutes later and with a
thank-you pat, he disappeared inside as well.

Then Mona emerged.

'You go home and get some rest,' one of the doctors told
her.

We waited for a bit and I heard Laila screaming away
inside. It sounded like bloody murder.

'She's refusing the epidural,' Tina said, emerging from
nowhere. 'Sometimes Laila can be so obstinate!'

We stood around for a bit and Mona covered her ears with
every scream.

'You should go,' Tina told her sympathetically. 'No point
panicking right now.'

Mona

'Too bad your baby shower didn't work out,' I told Tina right before leaving, trying to distract myself from the screaming.

She blinked at me and then realisation dawned upon her. Of course, now with the baby already here, it was too late for the shower.

I turned to Ramit. 'Tina's been planning one for this weekend. For Laila.'

'I had caterers booked,' Tina said with dismay. Then she snapped her fingers. 'I'm going to convert it to a welcome-home party for the baby.'

She immediately pulled out her phone and started barking orders. Ramit and I left.

'I'm not sure Laila will like that,' I told Ramit as we drove back home.

'What?'

'Tina's sent a text on the Laila Baby Shower group, saying that as Laila has gone into pre-term labour – which she hasn't really, because she's thirty-four weeks and it does qualify as full-term technically – she wants to convert the baby shower to a welcome party. I'm sure Laila will not be pleased to walk into a house full of people!'

'You should tell Tina that.'

'What? And have her cancel the catering and decorators and tell all the high flying page-three type people she's already blocked the date with that the party is off? That's like a death wish.'

Then Ramit and my phones buzzed at the same time.

It's a girl!

Ramit

And the rest of the evening, Mona sulked.

'I should be the one having the baby first, not Laila!' she kept muttering.

If the morning full of panic didn't induce labour, I don't think anything will. I decided to be a supportive husband nonetheless and stroked her hair till she fell asleep.

Mona

All the love I've been feeling for Laila has suddenly vanished. Now all I can think of is how competitive she was by having this baby before me and obviously had their wedding-night sex only to induce labour. I steal a glance at Ramit but he's already snoring away.

It was a miracle we conceived this baby in the first place!

Week 40

You will meet your baby any day now

Mona

Seriously? No sign of my labour starting any time.

We're at the hospital and Tina is complimenting Laila on doing this without an epidural.

Laila looks like a bloody diva. She's in this gorgeous floral gown and her hair is pulled back in a perky ponytail with a shiny scrunchie.

'I was dilating so fast I'm not sure they could have given me one in any case.'

'How is the baby doing?' Tina asks.

'Out of the NICU now. So excited to have her in our room.'

Since the baby was born a little early, she had to be under observation for the first twenty-four hours.

'Here she comes, after her bath.'

I turn to the little cradle being wheeled in, prepared to coo about how cute she is.

But oh! She's all pink and skinny and wrinkly and puffy-eyed and has these white acne type stuff all over her face and has a pretty strange looking nose.

Shashi and Laila and even Tina are cooing at the baby as if she's the prettiest thing they've seen! Are they blind? I think

Tina is just being artificial and can't possibly feel love for this baby. Laila is just blinded by her agonizing labour. And Shashi, well, he's a lawyer. He knows how to lie.

Before I know it, Shashi hands the baby over to me. It's then that I realize I don't even know how to hold a newborn. I coo along with them and wish someone would take the baby back from me but they're chatting away amongst themselves.

'Feeding time!' some doctor announces, walking in with a wide smile.

'Oh, I've already started lactating,' Laila says as she, much to my horror, starts to undo her buttons.

I'm just so glad Ramit isn't here to die of embarrassment. I hand over the baby and rush towards the door even as Shashi and Tina stand around to watch.

'Why don't you stay on, Mona? It will be good practice to see what you're in for?' Tina suggests with a naughty smile. I try to giggle to cover up for my nervousness as I see a white boob emerge from Laila's gown. I look away quickly and make a hasty exit. These people have no sense of privacy at all!

Ramit

I picked up Mona from the hospital and dropped in to say hello to the new parents. I have to say newborn babies are strange-looking. I mean, given how great-looking the parents are, this baby looks rather, um, not great.

Mona was fuming away as we drove off. I'm guessing it was because she is still very much pregnant while Laila isn't. But turns out, I'm wrong.

Mona

'Who does she think she is calling her daughter Adriana! That's a foreign name! It'll embarrass her all her life, that name. Adriana Sachdev!'

Ramit

Mona sat up in bed all night. At first, I thought it was another acidity attack but turns out she was still obsessing about Laila's baby-naming antics.

'Adriana! Of all names, they picked Adriana!'

Decided to leave Mona to her madness and went off to sleep.

She woke me up at 3:53 a.m. and declared that if we have a daughter, she will be called Natalia and if it's a boy, he'll be called Zayn.

Who does she think she's giving birth to? Some teenybopper popstar?

Mona

Uff! So sick of this endless waiting. And everyone keeps asking me how I'm still pregnant, like I'm choosing this!

Even Suhani bua, who till last week had sounded doomful about pre-term labour, calls me up today and sounds doomful about *not* going into labour.

'Is there even a baby inside you!'

'Bua, I'm 82 kilos! There better be a baby inside me!'

'82 kilos! Mona! That's too much! When I had Shubh I was 65 kilos max. What have you done to yourself? That's why you haven't gone into labour. Please go to the doctor immediately!'

All these years I thought the Deols were bad. Turns out the only reason I've been able to adjust with them is because I had been dealing with the cracked Mathur family all my life!

Week 41

Don't fret – you won't be pregnant forever

Mona

I'm going to be pregnant forever! That's just how it is! I'm in my forty-first week now!

Ten missed calls a day from Suhani bua.

Twenty calls a day from Mummy. Like we'll forget to inform her when I go into labour.

No calls from Mom because she's here with us now, her tea-party obligations over.

No calls from Shania because she's too busy setting up her marriage counselling website.

Ramit

I decide to accompany Mona on her next appointment with Dr Mehak. I am going to be stern and ask the doctor when the baby is arriving.

Dr Mehak spends some time examining Mona and then says, 'You know, I thought you'd come to me weeks ago. But since it hasn't happened and now you're overdue, why don't you just come in tonight?'

So much for my practiced speech.

353

We leave the clinic and I call Mummy. She and Papa are getting on the next flight.

Mona

You know how they show in all the movies that the woman goes into labour and instantly just knows it? Like her water breaks and everyone has to race her to the hospital at top speed, knocking off people in wheelchairs on the road and dashing into hospital lobbies and all that? A bit like Laila's labour, really.

But here are Ramit and me, with Ramit driving at snail-speed to the hospital at midnight. There's no hurry whatsoever, no drop in the position of the baby, no dilation, no nothing.

My labour has to be induced since the baby has decided to stay close to my heart – literally. He hasn't even come down. Who is *that* lazy!

The mothers wanted to accompany us but I told them to let the process start at least. I'm not sure why Dr Mehak has asked us to come in at midnight. Maybe she likes delivering kids at night so that she can be at the clinic during the day.

Anyway, here we are, glamourlessly standing at the fancy T&T hospital reception with our suitcases. I'm a bit embarrassed to admit that I couldn't get my body to work the normal way and actually have to be induced.

Laila very kindly messaged, saying that inducing labour is normal and I shouldn't panic about it, but she's one for saying that.

Then Ramit tells me he is taking a couple of days off work to help out with the baby and I look around for a sharp object to break his head with for suggesting two days of paternity leave. Two days. He says its company policy. He runs the company!

Ramit

We were accompanied to a really fancy room and the doctor on duty flipped through Mona's papers. She then looked at Mona's stomach and pronounced that the baby was still quite high. As if we didn't know.

Mona was handed some sort of gown to change into but she reappeared from the bathroom and called the nurse.

'Can I have another one? This one is torn from the back.'

After a bit of a confusing exchange, Mona realized that the gowns were meant to be open at the back.

A second nurse entered the room just after that, and turns out, Mona needed an enema. I was told to leave the room.

Glad to oblige!

Mona

The doctor on duty examined me and put me on IV and asked me to put some medicine under my tongue.

Then we heard a bloodcurdling scream from the other room.

Ramit and I looked at each other in panic.

My BP shot up instantly and the nurse told me to 'Kip calm.'

An hour later, I still couldn't feel too much. Just a few Braxton Hicks kind of spasms. I asked the doctor on duty if my labour had started. She looked at some machine I was strapped to and said, 'Yes. Decent levels of pain.'

I heard another scream from the adjoining room. Didn't understand what the big deal was.

Ramit took out his phone to work again but I glared at him so he quickly put it away. Then he decided to take a tour of the room. He came to the bed and started studying all the fancy buttons and made a move to press one. I glared at him again so he walked off.

Then he started inspecting all the cabinets across the room and opening all the drawers. Uff!

Why can't he just sit down and wait patiently. Like me!

Ramit

Three hours later, we decided to watch a movie on the telly in the room.

I boldly told the parents not to come till the doctor told us it was time, to which both the mothers grumbled, but I'm going to enjoy the last of whatever little peace is left in my life.

We settle on *Andaz Apna Apna*.

Three more hours later, no baby.

Mona

Dr Mehak walked into the room at 6 a.m., followed by a whole group of doctors. She was glamorously dressed in a purple dress and bright amethyst jewellery, as if she'd come in straight from a night of partying.

'You're still smiling,' she commented briskly.

She did a quick internal examination – there's no sense of shame and privacy left in me any more – in front of all the other doctors. I can now imagine why Laila wasn't ashamed of pulling out her boob in front of all of us to feed her baby.

'Dr Tullika,' Dr Mehak said crossly. 'She has hardly dilated. I saw her like this two weeks ago.' She tutted loudly and pushed some fingers into me.

I felt something ooze out of my body. I wondered if it was the baby or whether I'd peed.

And then realized she had broken my water.

'Any time now,' I heard Dr Mehak say as she walked out of the labour room. And then I heard another familiar voice floating in. 'Oh my God! I love the necklace you're wearing, doctor! I'm Shania, Mona's sister.'

And then the woman next door shrieked again.

Ramit

The mothers, fathers and Shania have arrived.

The mothers looked like they'd been up all night sulking about not being allowed to come earlier. The fathers looked like they'd been up all night drinking.

They all walked in excitedly and immediately began fussing over Mona.

Security threw them out. Apparently we were being so noisy that the woman in labour next door couldn't be heard.

Mona

Really don't know what the big deal is with all the screaming. What the doctor had called a good amount of pain had been so very bearable for me. Gosh, I must be some sort of superwoman!

The doctor asked me if I needed an epidural but I said no. If Laila could do without it, so could I.

The mothers were taking turns being in the room with me. I overheard a bit of the catfight the mothers had outside on who would come in first. Looks like the ex-principal won.

Ramit

Did I hear Mummy right?

Mona

Did I hear Ramit's Mummy right?

Suddenly the contractions felt much sharper. I had a bad one and waited for it to pass before I grabbed Ramit's arm and hissed at him.

'What did Mummy say? The bheed is here?'

'Now, now, Mona …' Ramit pacified me just as Mummy's comforting strokes on my back stopped and I caught her staring at me.

'Bheed? *Bheed*? Ramit, did Mona just call the cousins …'

Holy Shit! I said that in front of Mummy. Why was she still there?

Ramit was escorting her out of the room. 'Mummy, that's not what she meant. I mean …'

'Bheed?' she asked again, shocked. 'If Bade Papa hears that …'

I don't know if it was the shock of shocking Mummy or me being in real, actual labour, but I felt a massive spasm and everything went dark.

Ramit

Mona's contractions had suddenly gotten quite bad. She seemed to be passing out. And I had to get rid of the cousins.

Spent forty-five minutes shooing off the bheed from the labour room waiting area. Mona would kill me if she found out that all the Deols of Delhi *and* Amritsar had landed up to see her push. Moved everyone to the reception and created so much commotion that a staff member asked me if there was a film shooting going on. Finally managed to move the bheed to the cafeteria.

Returned to find Shania prancing around the room excitedly and … Oh God. She had taken a selfie with Mona writhing in pain in the background. Mona asked me to throw her out.

Sent her off and went down once again to convince the bheed to leave as it would take a while and just then, got an alert that Mona was officially in labour.

When I reached the labour room, the woman next door was shouting away again. Much worse this time. I only hoped … oh shit!

That screaming lady was Mona.

Mona

The mothers were bickering … over my pregnant body! Over my freaking contractions!

I think I yelled some expletives. They both looked shocked.

They ran out looking for Ramit.

And then I saw what my mother was wearing.

Ramit

Mona was abusing the shit out of everyone.

She said she wanted the epidural. Now.

I didn't know what to make of it. She had said no to the epidural earlier and now they told her it was too late to get one. If there was a vase by her bedside, she would have smashed it into their head. Or mine.

And she was in so much pain and so tired, she kept passing out every five minutes, awakening only to scream with a contraction. Except when she spotted Shania by her side. Somehow she found a fresh burst of energy to pull her in close and say, 'Shania, phoo phoo phoo, what on earth is Mom wearing!'

Mona

My contractions tripled simply at the sight of my mother. She was wearing a frock. That's correct! No other way of describing it. It was a goddamn yellow full-on frock with frills and everything! She thought she could pass it off as a kurta by teaming it with purple slacks, but she wasn't fooling anyone!

Ramit

Outside the room, Mom was giving it off to Shania.

'What do you mean the sight of me is inducing her labour! How dare you! I'm her mother!'

Then Mona's Dad appeared and asked me if I would like to join him and my father for a drink! A drink! At this hour! Of course I could use a drink, or ten, but to even ask me to step out with them …

And then Mummy walked in gleefully, announcing that Rina maasi was here.

'Now everything will be fine!' Mummy said, clapping her hands happily. 'Rina is a cardiologist,' she told Mona's mother. 'Now we have a doctor in our midst. Nothing to worry about!

'She's a cardiologist! We're in a maternity hospital!' I finally snapped, 'We have nothing to worry about, anyway. Dr Mehak is very well renowned.'

Mummy gave me her cold, principal-like stare. 'Mona has been in labour for nine hours. I believe something is terribly wrong and we need a doctor in the family to …'

I would have argued with her but suddenly, I took count of the faces in the room. Mom, Mummy, Dad, Papa, Shania, me. So who exactly was in there with Mona?

Mona

When Mummy walked out in a hurry, I assumed it was to send Ramit in. So what was goddamn Roshini-I-shat-on-the-labour-table-Roshan doing there?

Ramit

I'd expected Mona to be a lot angrier when I rushed in to be by her side.

'Bhaiya, this is a lady's job. Don't worry. You take it easy and sit outside.' Mona looked at her as if she would kill her, so I insisted I wanted to stay there with my wife and she could leave, please.

'Ramit, I need an epidural. And I'm too tired. I can't …' she let out a loud screech.

I patted her hand. 'It's all right. I'll just go speak to the doctor again.'

'Keep your bheed out of here!' she shouted as I ran out.

Mona

I ask Ramit to stay and whose faces appear by my side? The mothers.

'Mona, you don't need that epidural,' Mom told me.

'You'll regret it. Your back will ache all your life,' Mummy said.

'This is only a matter of a few minutes. Listen to Ramit's mother. The epidural will hurt you all your life.'

'Yes, beta. Women have had babies naturally for years. Go natural.'

'Laila didn't take the epidural either.'

'You can do it.'

The bickering mothers had united against me! Now they drop their differences? To torture me!

I had an awful contraction right then and I screamed but then I also cried loudly just for effect. I needed that bloody epidural! And I didn't bloody care what anyone said.

Ramit

The junior doctor was shaking her head. 'She's already 8 cm dilated. We can't give her the epidural now.'

Mona was passing out so I squeezed her hand and said, 'It's okay, baby. You're almost there.'

She huffed and puffed before passing out again.

She looked so pale and fatigued. I wondered if she was going to die.

Mona

Dr Mehak finally decided to grace us with her presence after I'd been in labour for eternity.

Ramit said it had been eleven hours but it felt like years. I don't know how long I'd been moving in and out of consciousness and how long I'd been screaming and trembling with pain.

She was in blue overalls but still had a long string of blue stones hanging from her neck. She has jewellery to match with her hospital outfit! I wish my mom would learn from her … wait! I was in freaking labour! Why was I thinking about my mother's fashion sense?

Some assistant doctors grabbed hold of my legs and unceremoniously yanked them into stirrups.

'It's time!' Dr Mehak announced.

'But I need the epidural!' I screamed.

They looked at me like I was crazy.

'Push Push Push Push Push!' I heard them all yelling at me together.

So I yelled a loud, 'YEEEEAAAAHHHHHHH' right back at them.

'Shut your mouth, Mona!' Dr Mehak scolded me. I was so taken aback. 'Save you energy for the pushing!' she added.

After the contraction subsided and I was ready to nod off with fatigue, I heard Ramit smooth my hair and say, 'You'll be okay. It'll be over soon.'

Before I could thank him, another freaking contraction burst through me.

This time I tried not to scream but a loud piercing shriek filled the room.

'Mona! You have to shut your mouth!' Dr Mehak reprimanded, without looking at me.

'Um … that was the husband,' I heard the assistant tell her.

Ramit

Embarrassing much … but the way she dug her fingers into my arm I thought she'd pull out a large chunk of flesh.

Yes, I know having your flesh pulled out isn't as bad as pushing a baby out of your, you know, but it still hurt. Badly.

Mona

I can't remember how long that went on or what exactly happened but somewhere, I passed out again. When I woke up, things were quieter and I heard someone laugh. I think it was Ramit. I heard a small cry. One fainting spell later, a grumpy looking child was thrust on to my chest. Another fainting spell later I felt a needle piercing through me and I realized it was all done.

'What is it?' I managed to croak.

'It's your baby,' a nurse said.

Obviously it's my baby! Do they think I pushed out my brain with the child?

'But what is it?' I insisted.

'Oh. It's a boy.'

Before my eyes shut, I saw Ramit's face shining down at the thing wrapped in green.

Ramit

Texted all the cousins and asked them to leave, since Mona would take some time to settle down.

I was just about to go check the room they were shifting Mona to when I bumped into Dr Mehak.

'I have to tell you something about the baby's private parts,' she told me.

I swear my heart dropped to my knees and all of Mummy and Mom's warnings came flashing into my mouth.

I cleared my throat and found my timid voice. 'Um, is it about the ...'

'Penis. Yes,' she confirmed.

'There's a tiny birth mark on it,' she said matter-of-factly. 'I just wanted to let you know lest you worry about it later.'

The baby

Mona

People have left the room now, finally. The nurse has brought in the baby for the night. Thankfully, it's asleep. I wish they would keep him in the nursery tonight. I'm exhausted. And the way Ramit is fluffing up his pillows on the sofa-cum-bed at the other end of the room, I'm pretty sure he's going to be good for nothing. But I couldn't let the mothers stay. My patience with them is currently non-existent.

There was just so much happiness everywhere. The fathers were so excited – though they looked a little drunk. The bheed all stopped by, claiming they'd just happened to drop in, though I have a nagging feeling they'd been here all night. The phone calls haven't stopped coming. Suhani bua had no doomful story to share. And Shania hasn't said a single nasty thing about the baby. In fact, she's been cooing at it and clicking pictures like mad. Maybe that's her new phase. Photography.

The baby is asleep and Ramit is lying down with his eyes closed. But there's something that's been nagging me all day that I have to tell Ramit.

'Ramit …' I whisper, so as to not wake up the baby.

369

'Ramit.' I whisper a bit more loudly. Nothing.

'Ramit!'

I consider throwing a pillow at him just when the nurse walks in to administer some medicines. *That* wakes him up.

'What?' he asks, judging my expression.

Ramit

To tell you the truth, I'm a little afraid of Mona, ever since I saw her bearing her fangs while pushing out that … purple human being. So when I see her looking at me angrily, I almost run out of the door. Then I remember all those books asking me to be a supportive husband and I get myself to sit by her bedside and hug her by the shoulder.

'I have something to confess,' she says softly.

She stays silent for a long time and suddenly I feel more awake. Is she going to now tell me that the baby is not mine? Is it … Shashi's? Has he impregnated all the women around him?

'I know I'm supposed to feel all the maternal love oozing out of me the minute I hold the baby, but I'm just … I don't feel anything.'

I hold her for quite a while.

'Why is this child so … purple?' she says finally.

I laugh so loudly, the baby wakes up and screeches and oh my god, what a screech it is!

So we stay up all night.

Mona

We don't know what the hell to do with the baby. I try feeding it and it hurts like hell. We finally call in the nurse who takes the baby out for a diaper change. When she brings him back in, he's fast asleep.

I'm now checking WhatsApp while Ramit snores on his couch. I scroll through all the pictures taken in the last thirty-six hours and my heart sinks below sea level.

I'd always thought I'd look fresh and happy and glowing, holding the tiny, fatty baby in my arms, dressed in blue overalls. But here I am, in a faded purple, polka-dotted nightgown, my boobs pouring out from every corner and my hair dishevelled. Not at all like Laila and her shiny scrunchie.

Ramit

Woken up by a nervous nurse who comes screaming in to announce, 'Daacter is here, daacter is here!'

Dr Mehak floats in with a bouquet of assistants.

'How're you doing?' she asks.

'Very tired,' I reply, rubbing my eyes. She gives me an amused look. Apparently the question was meant for Mona.

'Dr Mehak,' Mona says. 'My stomach is still so huge. Are you sure there isn't another baby in there?'

Mona

Dr Mehak may say it's normal and it'll take a while for the uterus to settle down, but I don't remember seeing Laila looking pregnant after Adriana was born.

Laila walks in a little later, her tiny baby wrapped in her arms wearing.

'Here, beta,' Mom says magnanimously, 'place little Andrea next to the baby on the sofa so that we can take a picture of them together.'

'She's Adriana, not Andrea,' I correct her.

'Oh that's even lovelier than Andrea. I loved the name! Mona, have you decided finally what to name the baby?'

'We could call him Chooey till then,' Mummy pipes in. 'He's such a little chooey, isn't it? Isn't it? Isn't it?' she starts cooing at the baby.

I wanted to barf. Chooey! If they shorten the pet name further it'll be Choo! Choo for ...

Ramit appears by my bedside to show me a picture of the two babies he's clicked. My heart sinks further. I have given birth to a mouse, compared to Laila's fluffed-up little girl. I have to say a couple of weeks and her baby already looks beautiful and not how it did on the first day. While mine ...

Then Adriana starts crying so I panic that Laila will pull one boob out in front of everyone and feed her. But she whips out a bottle and both mothers immediately gasp.

'Already on the bottle?'

'I pumped it, Aunty. It's not really a top feed. Don't worry.'

We will be justifying our choices and actions to total strangers a whole lot more in the future, I realize with dismay.

Five minutes later, here I am, feeding the baby in front of Laila and the mothers and my pink-eared husband, who's glued to his phone.

Ramit

Shania's cooing at the baby, rocking it to sleep.

'They're so tiny, so delicate. I want one too. But, I guess I'll probably need to get married for that and I'm not sure if that's really worth it.'

'What do you mean by 'probably'? Don't you give me a heart attack, young lady!' Mona's mom takes off on her.

I turn back to the form I'm filling.

'Mona,' I asked her tentatively, 'I need to put down the baby's name on the birth certificate form.'

I am praying she's dropped the idea of Zayn.

'Of course we do,' she replies cheerfully. 'He's going to be Kabir Deol.'

Kabir

My God it's bright out here! I can barely open my eyes. And someone has had the bright idea to strangle me with this swaddle cloth. I really need to stretch but there's no place in this blanket. I had a lot more place inside the dark cell I could float around in.

Anyway, coming out into this brightness has been very exhausting. So I've slept most of the day. Every time I opened my eyes, there was a new face shining down at me saying stuff like 'Golu-Molu, Chhotu-Motu.' It's like everyone has to speak in rhymes and rhymes alone.

I have warmed up to Round-Face, of course. She smells sweet and feels like a giant mattress. And the bespectacled bony guy is okay too, except he bounces me around a bit too much. I also like the other pretty girl who keeps discussing plans of taking me to some ashram and taking me trekking and I thought we were friends till she blinded me yesterday with some sort of flashlight. I told her off then and it took a whole lot of hands to calm me down after that.

I've also been sung to a lot – especially by tall blunt cut woman and short dishevelled hair woman who keep saying

Naaaani- Daaaadi, training me to say that as my first word but I'm smarter than that. Plus their singing sucks! It sounds nothing like Remix 90s by DJ Suketu that I was made to listen to in the dark cell.

But my favourite is Angel-Face. She smells sweet, she glows at me and has this husky voice I remember hearing a lot in the cell. And all was well till she placed me next to this giant pink ball of fur who scowled at me immediately and I returned the favour. Not sure it registered because my face muscles aren't working very well.

Ew, you look like a mouse! she had the audacity to tell me.

And you look like a giant cotton candy, I bit right back.

I'd rather be a cotton candy than be a squeaky mouse.

Oh really? Because your voice is really sounding a whole lot more mouse-like than mine is.

Oh really? Would you like to hear what my real voice sounds like? Take this! And she screamed.

How dare she! I gave it right back at her. We volleyed another three rounds, taking it several pitches higher every time, when Angel-Face quickly took her away and I was passed on to Round-Face, but we both continued our verbal assault till the massive ball of pink fur was taken out of my sight. It was sad to see Angel-Face go with her but we'll just count it as collateral damage.

I hope she isn't coming back.

Anyway, all that lung exercise was exhausting. Time for another nap.

Acknowledgments

I have *so* many people to thank for this book.

My amazing husband, Moksh, who dutifully reads whatever I write, compliments it sufficiently and encourages me to do more of it. Thank you for telling me to pursue what I love. And thank you for being the inspiration behind workaholic Ramit (haha!).

My mum, for always telling me she's proud of me and for giving me the time to hammer away at my laptop by patiently looking after my brats as they turn her house upside-down.

My mum-in-law, for her constant encouragement and for calling dibs on playing the role of the mother-in-law if the book is ever made into a movie!

My sister, Seemeen, my biggest pillar of strength, for believing in me and for guffawing madly at the manuscript for days.

My brother-in-law, Amar, for promising to secretly buy lots of copies of the book and gifting them to all his friends. I'm sure a book on pregnancy will make for great reading for a bunch of CEO-type people.

My niece, Kyrah, for agreeing to be my official photographer and for very kindly blaming the light rather than my face for not getting it right a hundred times.

My cousin, Ayesha, for being the inspiration behind Shania. For being crazy but lovable. But crazy.

My various lifelines: The Burneys, the Chopras, the Khans, the Wadhwas, my Giggles, my Secret Society, my Usual Gang and my very own grammar coach from Chennai – thank you for your enthusiasm. You guys are the best!

Thank you, Yashodhara Lal Sharma, for being my mentor, in so many ways, always.

Thank you, Harper Collins India – Swati Daftuar for telling me you loved the book, Arcopol Chaudhuri for your patience with my childlike excitement, and Diya Kar, for believing in this story.

Thank you, my 'good news', Zayn and Iram, for bringing such incredible amount of joy to our lives every single day, and without whom I would have never realized the hilarity of the journey.

Thank you, Dad, for being my guiding star, for passing on your love for writing and for watching over me always.

And finally, thank you dear reader, for picking up and reading this fairly fat book. I hope it brought you a nice, hearty laugh.